TH

By

Rita Ariyoshi

THE MANGO QUEEN OF WAIKIKI

By

Rita Ariyoshi

 Savant Books and Publications Aignos Publishing

Savant Books and Publications Honolulu, HI, USA

2024

ALSO BY RITA ARIYOSHI

Fiction: *Lion's Way*

Non-Fiction: *Maui on My Mind, Hula is Life, National Geographic Traveler Hawaii*

ABOUT THE AUTHOR

Short fiction by Rita Ariyoshi has appeared in consumer magazines and literary journals such as *The Missouri Review, The MacGuffin, Literary Mama, Hawaii Pacific Review, Witness* and *Rosebud.* Her awards include a Pushcart Prize; grand prize in the National Steinbeck Center short story competition; first prize in fiction, Japanophile Press; first prize in fiction Ian MacMillan short story competition. Ariyoshi's previous novel, LION'S WAY (Savant Publications, 2022) earned her the Elliot Cades Award for Literature from the Hawaii Literary Arts Council and the University of Hawaii. Her non-fiction books and articles in *National Geographic Traveler, Travel and Leisure, Islands,* and others, have also garnered numerous awards. She was the founding editor of *Aloha, The Magazine of Hawaii and the Pacific,* and served as editor-in-chief for more than a decade. She lives in Honolulu.

Published in the USA by Savant Books and Publications LLC
P.O. Box 19182 Honolulu, HI 96817   USA
http://www.savantbooksandpublications.com

Printed in the USA Edited by: Vern Turner

Cover images from: www.canva.com Cover by Kendrick
Simmons

DEDICATION
To Lorelai Aki

CHAPTER ONE

In which the ancient Mr. Lau Yi Ching covets the Mango Queen's mangoes, she goes dancing at the Pagoda Hotel with an old war hero and reaches too high.

In the El Nino year of 1998, the mangoes came two months early, in May instead of July.

That's how the accident happened. Nature was out of whack. Her orthodoxy of flower and fruit and harvest, of bursting, ripening and rot, had lapsed. Mango flowers bloomed in January while the Christmas poinsettias were still ablaze, while the plumeria branches were naked of leaves and before the winter rains sent boulders the size of Toyotas over the waterfalls of Ma`akua, Manoa and Kaliuwa`a. People were unprepared for their seasonal allergies and many skipped them altogether. Chutney makers hurried to get organized early, clattering about their kitchens with empty baby-food and mayonnaise jars, performing the mysteries of paraffin, feeling rushed, peeved, and in awe as before a great storm.

Yes, the cosmos definitely had a kink in it that

year. Many said it was because the millennium was hurtling toward a supine and puzzled world as if it were a terrible shock and people had not had a thousand years to get ready for the parties, doomsday criers, alien visitations and media frenzy.

Melba Yamada Matsuda did not concern herself with such matters. She was raised on Zen and came of age to the tune of Doris Day warbling *"Que sera, sera ..."* She figured she was as sunny as she ought to be, and making slow but certain progress on her serenity issues by simple, ruthless repression of memory and its acolyte emotions. She was glad to be beyond the age of reproduction with its mess and emissions, glad to have come out the other end of passion with a paid-up mortgage. When airwave prophets with Southern accents shouted, "Prepare. The end times are at the door," she harumphed in scorn and changed the channel. While television arrayed before its calamity-besotted audience, an extraordinary fluorescence of serial killers, killer parents, famine, flood, and fire, Melba did her housework. She hummed as pandemic plagues were promised. It was only a question of time until sinister vapors leaked out of a secret Siberian laboratory, or a jet streaked out of Africa carrying a pathogen-riddled host in the early, subversive grip of *ebola*, Nile fever, anthrax or vivid new mutants causing bleeding from the eyeballs and the brain to go to curry on the way to London, Washington, Tokyo or New York.

     Catastrophes were as common on the nightly news as desperate new traffic schemes for the H-1 Freeway, Honolulu-bound from Ewa. There were particularly local omens, too. The eerie drum-like mating calls of the *bufo* were seldom heard in the Hawaiian night, even in the damp reaches of valleys so deep they never saw a sunrise or a sunset. It had been ages since anyone had flattened the toad on the road or had to scoop its luminous choking strands of 100,000 eggs from koi ponds in the morning. "This is a sign," the primly dressed door-to-door salvation dispensers proclaimed with palmy smiles as they passed out their Doomsday tracts, "'The disappearance of amphibians. It's in the Bible." Their eyes glittered with the thrill of the impending Apocalypse, to which they, of course, would be immune, armored as they were with the breastplate of The Only Truth. Even parlor agnostics, who had never given credence to the phenomenon of El Nino, who if they thought of it at all, regarded it warily as another conspiracy of the CIA or an international banking cabal. They were taking a second look at the Second Coming, at global warming, the loss of the ozone layer, and the probability of a random meteor hit obliterating life as we know it. Many were armed to the teeth.

Melba had more important matters on her mind. She sat in her big wicker armchair on the lava-rock porch of her weathered yellow house in Kaimuki, her back propped by the hard little fake needlepoint pillow that said, "I love Grandma." For more than a month now, she had been regarding her mango tree growing pendulous with fruit out of season. "Tomorrow," she sighed heavily. Her knees ached from too much gardening -- and she had a dinner to face that night.

Melba was a small, thin woman with surprisingly athletic suppleness for her sixty-eight years. In fact, she was so trim and agile, that if she bothered to dye her hair, which was still largely black anyway thanks to eating seaweed daily, she would appear a decade younger. Perhaps without glasses, she could be two decades younger, certainly young enough to be carded on senior citizen discount Tuesdays at Daiei Market.

She glanced at the long eggplants she had just picked, resting like a nest of indigo snakes in the basket beside her, next to yesterday's glass of water with a couple of black ants swimming tired circles in it, and concluded, "One harvest a day is enough. The mangoes will have to wait until tomorrow."

The mango tree and Melba shared a long history. In fact, because of that tree, and, of course, her dragon mother, the youthful Melba had agreed, with a mixture of begrudged affection and theatrical deep-sighing resignation, but certainly nothing approaching lust, to marry reliable, local *nisei,* Shuzo Matsuda, instead of a certain *haole* soldier passing through on his way to war in Korea, a soldier she imagined, for some time, even years into her marriage, was the love of her life. She had met Shuzo in botany lab at the University of Hawaii. He had presented a paper on an experiment in which he made sixteen successful grafts onto a common mango stock. Melba was intrigued and insisted on seeing this unique tree. It was love at first sight. Love of the man came much later.

The tree was now down to seven kinds of mango. Melba lost one grafting for every year of her widowhood, even with all the care she lavished on the tree, faithfully fertilizing and watering. If she lived long enough, Shuzo's tree would be back to common roots. Mango trees are like family trees. They have brief moments of glory and then, in spite of care, it gets down to simple brute endurance, as if all of evolution is aimed at one brilliant generational moment.

She put her feet upon her weeding stool, prepared to pleasantly worry awhile. Benign neglect might be a worthy strategy in both trees and grown children. Too much care resulted in stunting.

Nobody could accuse Melba of parental

indulgence. She couldn't afford to be overly involved in her son's life. First, Lance was a policeman with an exacting schedule and worrisome exposure to danger. A routine traffic stop might turn into *Gunfight at the O.K. Corral.* Second, Lance's wife, Kathleen, was *haole,* meaning she might have a good heart but she didn't understand anything. They had two sons, but it was their daughter Rosemary, the girl of large black eyes and thick *ehu* hair, who was the one vivifier of Melba's emotions. *Que sera, sera* did not work with this granddaughter. Life must be good to this child, or life would have Melba to answer to.

Melba's daughter Cindy required no such expenditure of anxiety - even though she was pregnant again - since she was thousands of miles away. She lived in Singapore with a maid for the house, an amah for the children, a driver for the Mercedes and a Harvard-educated husband to pay for it all. Melba trusted implicitly the hygiene of maternity wards in a country that clipped the beards off foreigners at the airport and snipped the kisses right out of major motion pictures.

Renee, now, was another matter. It took effort to keep from despairing of this daughter. In fact, it took aggressive annoyance to deal with her – that – and, if honesty permitted, meanness. A mother cannot, in good conscience, appear to condone certain behavior, even though she might have once been the despair of her own mother.

Melba scratched her back on the back of the chair and looked up to see Mr. Lau Yi Ching, thin as a stick and older than Earth, crossing toward her. He was on his way home laden with plastic bags of fish, choi-sum, green onion, and god-knows-what from Maunakea Street – ginseng tea for his brain, lizard tail for his joints, snake tonsil for virility. He paused by her croton hedge with, as always, an admirable mischief in his rheumy eyes. Also in this moment, he displayed open, naked greed and longing as he looked at her mango tree. "You pick em soon." It wasn't an order or a question. It was a recognition that they both knew the time had come, the exact and precise time to pick mango.

"Tomorrow."

Mr. Lau Yi Ching probably had the taste of pickled mango already upon his raptor tongue. He smiled, nodded. He was ninety if he was a day. Possibly there was something to be said for his evil smelling little bundles.

"Rain," he said, gathering his bags of fungi and dried innards protectively to his chest as he hurried away with the delicate agility of a sugarcane spider.

Melba felt the cool mountain breath of the coming rain freshening her skin. Its fragrance preceded it, heavy with ginger and exhilaration, tangy with its own sweet stealth. It always rained when Melba planted seeds, as she did today. All she had to do was bring home a packet from Star Market and clouds gathered on the Ko`olau ridges. When she got out her trowel, they began to fill the green bowl of Palolo Valley, and by the time she covered the seeds in their furrows, the rain ghosted down Ninth Avenue, often in the gossamer company of rainbows. The shimmering, wind-blown curtain seemed to hesitate before her old yellow house, still lit by sunlight, dazzling to behold against a turbulent sky, and then the mist stole across the garden, gently sprinkling the seeds in their new beds, enticing them to yield to the pressure of the life coiled within them, thick white life pushing against hard nutty walls, heaving upward against earth and all the forces of gravity, slender and tender, seeking light, to become greenness, to bloom and feed, briefly splendidly, then bend and die. This day she had put in sunflowers, rows of them in front of the crotons. As far as she could recall, no one had ever planted sunflowers on Ninth Avenue, probably not in all of Kaimuki.

She left the rain and went inside to shower and blow-dry her hair for the Four-Four-Two dinner.

Kenji Kojima picked her up promptly at six o'clock. He was tall for his generation of Japanese, and had the unlined face of a man who, for most of his adult life, rose in the morning to find immaculate white jockey shorts neatly stacked in his dresser drawer, aloha shirts pressed and lined up by color on hangers in his closet, and his coffee freshly brewed. Widowhood had come as a shock, leaving him bewildered and bereft with a closetful of wrinkled shirts and drawers tumbling with balled up boxers. For Kenji, widowhood wasn't merely inconvenient. It was another shameful survival, World War II being the first. Solitude did not agree with him, but neither did disloyalty to the dead spouse. Polite, sweet, uncommitted, and unattainable, he was perfect for Melba.

She, on the other hand, was nothing like his deceased spouse. She was bossy, stubborn and emotionally distant. But she was a beauty and she kept him going with her plans, laughter and marching orders. He would be lost without her.

The only thing Melba disliked about Kenji was that he didn't lift his feet when he walked, as if he still wore G.I. boots in the snowy forests of Germany. She also wished for the flattery of a proposal so she could decline with a generous grace that would relieve them both.

The dinner was at the Pagoda Hotel set among the koi ponds. Melba could rely on the buffet: teriyaki chicken, sliced roast of beef au jus, *miso* soup, the good kind of *namasu* with crab meat, cold *somen*, *ogo* salad, and a mild, not too vinegary coleslaw. She could have as many desserts as she wanted, including soft-serve ice cream with hot fudge and colored sprinkles. When you no longer had passion, you were entitled to extra dessert.

In the two years that she had been seeing Kenji, Melba had gotten to know the families of the much-decorated Japanese-American veterans. Increasingly, the men showed up on the arms of doting daughters and sons as the years took a toll that even combat against the Nazis had been unable to exact. They came in their hats and insignia, and kept meeting because they needed each other as they needed no one else, for no one else carried in their dreams a specific knowledge of evil. In mixed company, the men never mentioned the war, and according to Kenji, seldom spoke of it even to each other. They had no words to tell their stories in either English or Japanese.

Maybe Melba's accident could be partially attributed to the dinner. Catastrophe can be contagious. Chablis doesn't help. At her age, she couldn't afford to lose a single brain cell to alcohol or anything else. Perhaps the Chablis slurped a balance cell, a small tidbit in the neighborhood of her inner ear, while she innocently raised her glass and poked daintily at the *ogo*

salad, her delicate, studied gestures reminding people
that she once wore a tiara, had been the University of
Hawaii *Ka Palapala* beauty queen and was now aging
well without benefit of cosmetic surgery.

The morning after the buffet dinner and glass of
Chablis, when Melba marched from her carport to the
mango tree, lugging her stepladder, she found herself
irritated by the tree's aberrant bloom. "It's not right," she
muttered. "Mangoes in May." She had no sense of
foreboding, although she would later imagine that she
did. She was simply resentful of this imposition placed
on her by nature's unpredictable fecundity. It was rather
like an unplanned pregnancy, annoying, but the results
would be worth it once the mess was cleaned up. She
thought of her children, who didn't deserve mangoes
because they never helped pick them, but who would get
them anyway because blood is thicker than gall.

She wedged the ladder firmly into the bare
ground in the thick shade of the old tree and rocked it
back and forth, testing its stability. She had a plastic
grocery bag looped over her arm and the pruning shears
on a string around her neck as she began to cautiously
climb the ladder. She stood for a moment in the dense
shade with the fullness of life all around her, the tree
groaning with heaviness, humming in secret,
conspiratorial female pleasure. She reached into the

leaves. Her fingers wrapped around the first blushing mango of this strange season. Its warm, golden skin, freckled with pink, orange and coral, deepened to purple and green on top where it leaked sticky sap. She paused, filled with gratitude. Then she cut the fruit from its long stem, feeling its smooth heft fall fully into her waiting hand.

After securing the first mango, she worked efficiently, the snip of her shears quite distinct in the temple of the tree. And then she saw, up high where sun beams pierced the canopy, deep in the dusty leaves, what she hadn't seen in years – a white Pirie mango, silvery in the sunlight like the skin of swimming fish. She stared at it. She thought that particular grafting had died years ago; was, in fact, the first to go, as if her husband had taken it with him along with his love when the cancer got him. El Nino must have resurrected it in much the same way it tricked the tree into this unseemly May flooziness.

She cautiously climbed up one more step, knowing as she did, that she was too high. The white mango glowed softly as a mid-day moon, lightly frosted in palest green, swaying on its stem. Her fingers jiggled it, but it was just a little too high to grab. She knew she should go down for the long bamboo mango picker, but instead she tugged on a bunch of leaves to pull the branch lower, and the next thing she knew, she was falling, surprised and furious, "What a stupid, stupid way to die." Simultaneously, she thought, "Was it like this for you, Papa? Why Papa?"

That's all she remembered.

CHAPTER 2

The Mango Queen is in a coma and has a near-death experience. In the bright light, Melba sees, instead of Jesus, the atomic bomb and her dead mother. She sees little difference.

There is nothing you can do when lying in bed in a coma. Melba reflected on her condition as an intermission, something like hurtling through the air on a plane trip. There you are, strapped in your seat with nothing holding you aloft but machinery and mystery. You are a resigned captive until it lands. Your basic needs are met. You are entertained with music in your headset and films edited for a general audience on the screen. Attendants bring you honeyed peanuts, trays of what appears to be food, and enough Coca Cola to float a canoe. You are beyond the reach of family. You cannot respond to their demands. Their dramas and head colds are distilled by distance and height. If the kitchen faucet has not been turned off, the newsboy not notified of your holiday, a middle-aged daughter living happily without a husband -- so be it. The umbilical cord is cut. Given long enough, it may wither to fragile string. The duty phone call. Mother's Day.

I'm sure I'm in a coma, an empty silent space, a place that should be terrifying, but isn't because I'm completely helpless. My life rests entirely in the hands of others while Death courts me. The dance that Death and I do is so intimate that trust, of necessity, blooms. It comes so naturally, so tenderly and inconspicuously, that I don't even notice its stealthy arrival, its reassuring tyranny. Trust the mechanic, trust the pilot, trust the doctor, trust the minimum-wage-health-care-professional in charge of drip feeding. There is no choice. Trust or be subdued, medication or handcuffs, one or the other. So complete and sweet is the surrender, that we need to be coaxed back from comas and vacations with entreaties and endearments, with obligations and half-forgotten imperatives, until the inexorable pull of home kicks in. Or else we might never return. We might remain in some alien paradise that tricks us into believing it is benign.

We may be led into a crowded landscape seeking ancients who look like us or a cousin. We may see the great white light people speak of, but for me that light turns out to be the atomic bomb that makes every ancestor before my mother faceless, nameless.

The light was so intense, Melba wondered that it did not consume her eyes. She stood transfixed before its magnificence, and then, shimmering in a soft place beyond the brilliance and out the other side of it, she saw a little green house deep in a green valley. A dog barked. Toads drummed their warty lust, and there, on the steps facing west into the light, shoulders straight as bamboo, a woman waited, trailing lotus flowers and regrets, staring as if she might, by sheer force of will, peer through the lurid brightness and find someone she knew. Her grief clouded around her.

The space between Melba and the woman was alive with the burning light, and with a vast and terrible anger. *Mother? Oka-san? Is that you?*

The woman did not turn her face.

I am alone, even though she is here. This is familiar.

My name is Melba Yamada Matsuda. I live in Kaimuki. Mr. Bill Clinton is president. Two plus two equals four.

CHAPTER THREE

In which the comatose Melba remembers the
Dauntless Dive Bomber and picks plumeria
blossoms. She is safe, but not for long. She buys
a name for her baby sister who is born too soon.

When Melba Yamada was ten years old, her best
friend, not counting Sweetie Waioli, was the mango tree
in the front yard of her small house in Kalihi Kai. She
could climb so high into the fruit tree and sit so still in its
branches that even when someone was standing directly
beneath, peering up into the dense dark leaves to find
her, they wouldn't see her. In the treetop, she was safe
from terrors she had not yet experienced, but sensed
sometimes in the cough of a parent or a sky gone dark in
the middle of day. Because she was so young, she was
free to hope without ridicule and intrusions of
impediments. The future was not confined to named
streets but sailed ahead with the clouds. Who will I be?
What will I do?

Carefully, with quick, skink-like moves, Melba
climbed up where the limbs swayed. It was dangerous to
go this high, but she was confident of the strength of her

tree. Also, she didn't weigh much. She was small for her age, but every inch was tough and sinewy, built for hard times and survival.

She sat in a crook of branches, feeling the rub of bark on bare brown legs and the flutter of breeze-stirred leaves. From here, she could look down on her neighborhood as she imagined it might look from an airplane. Unseen, she watched all the comings and goings, listened to dogs and roosters, to people calling to each other, each creature so important to itself, strutting, posturing and so entertaining. Melba saw who spat in the street when they thought no one was looking. She had their names. She saw the look of pain on Auntie Kapu's face as she walked heavily from side to side, supporting her great weight first on one swollen ankle and then the other. Auntie Kapu filled out her ample mu`umu`u all around. Her hips were of a truly awesome size and her *okole* was butter. Auntie Kapu stopped every so often to catch her breath, wipe her brow, and touch, as if for strength, the hibiscus garden in her greying hair, which was wound into a tight neat knot at the nape of her neck. When Auntie Kapu saw someone coming, she would pull herself into regal immensity, smile generously, whether she knew them or not, and greet them with, "Aloha."

If they were Hawaiian, they would respond,

"*Aloha no,* Auntie. *Pehea oe?*"

And she would nod. *"Maika`i."*

If they were Japanese, they would not speak, but bow their heads as slightly as good manners permitted, and hurry on. Melba knew all the subtle degrees of bowing, how to give slight in apparent humility.

If they were Chinese, they might very well respond to Auntie in Hawaiian because the Chinese came to Hawaii a while ago and they learned exactly what to do. They might inquire, if they knew her, "How you stay, Auntie?"

If they were *haole,* and a man, they might tip a hat. *Haoles* need hats because their skin gets *haole* rot in the sun. Melba had never seen a *haole* woman in this neighborhood and could not imagine one, in high heels with bobbed pale hair and a brooch on her dress, walking down the streets of Kalihi.

Not one of the passers-by, no matter who they were or how they answered, saw Auntie Kapu's pain. Nobody but Melba, looking down from the mango tree with the perspective of the Buddha, knew how much the Hawaiian lady hurt.

Melba also knew the sounds of the military airplanes that flew into Hickam, Pearl and Wheeler. When she heard the drone of an engine, she would close her eyes and listen carefully, deciding which plane it was, the beaky P-40 or the bulldog-faced Dauntless Dive Bomber. She would open her eyes, and be right. She was positive she knew more about airplanes than her brothers, Peter who just turned fifteen and thought that made him an expert on everything, and Raymond who read so much that at thirteen his eyes were already wrecked and he couldn't see the difference between an airplane and a mynah bird. Boys were dumb anyway.

Suddenly Melba heard the plane that made her heart flutter with pure joy and unutterable longing. She had been waiting for it, facing out to sea, and it was right on schedule. She always heard it before she saw it -- the China Clipper coming around Diamond Head. She loved the luxurious drone as it glided elegantly past Waikiki and over Honolulu Harbor. She saw its full-bellied bulk and duck-like pontoons wing past Kalihi Kai. High in the mango tree, she began to sing, "Far-away places, with strange sounding names, calling, calling – me." She drew out the notes dreamily, "Going to China, or maybe Siam ..." The plane descended low over Ke'ehi Lagoon in the final stretch toward Pearl Harbor. She pictured the excitement of the passengers looking out the windows as her ocean spread out below in the heavenly teals of a peacock's feathers. To their right they would gasp at Melba's brooding mountains, at the curtains of color hanging over the valleys where sunlit rain danced down in veils. She was as proud of her island, beautiful Oahu, as if it were a parent who spoke English.

She pictured the passengers sipping little cups of tea like the ladies and gentlemen in *Little Lord Fauntleroy,* which her blonde teacher, Mrs. Lane, was currently reading aloud to the class, a little each day. The China Clipper always seemed to pause over the water as if it did not want to leave the freedom of the sky. It hovered a moment as ducks do, inhaling the warm breath of the looming land, then skimmed the waves, white foam spraying up from the pontoons. The people on the pier would clap, the ukulele music would begin and the lei ladies would move out of the shade with their garlands of flowers draped over their arms. Highly buffed touring cars would whisk the bedazzled tea drinkers - by then up to their ears in flowers - to the pink Arabian corridors of the Royal Hawaiian Hotel or to the white wedding cake Moana where they would have more tea. Hours ago, they were someplace else. Now they were here. It was a wonder.

*

Melba's mother had a baby yesterday. She came home early from her job at Matsufuji-san's tofu factory, already in labor and worried because it was too soon. The baby died. Melba was sent to the Naming Lady with money in a red lee-see envelope and instructions to ask for a lower price for the baby's name, since it would be hardly used. Her father had argued against the expense as unnecessary since the baby was *ma`ke*-die-dead. Oka-san, for the first time that Melba could remember, dared to defy Oto-san. During and immediately after a birth is a woman's only time of advantage because she is doing something no man can do, no matter how powerful, cunning, or rich. She is bringing forth new life that has been formed of her blood and bones.

Melba ran all the way to the Naming Lady afraid her father might call her back as her mother's power waned. She arrived out of breath, clattering in her *geta* up the rickety wooden steps, and gasped out the story, aware of her important role in this domestic tragedy.

The Naming Lady was skinny and bent like a boomerang. Her ancient skin was so tight on her cheek bones it looked polished. She had named half the children in Kalihi and most in Chinatown. New parents came to her because they were Asian immigrants and they did not know which American names were good and which might be liabilities.

The Naming Lady took the red envelope, examined its contents, chewed her lips and asked "Dead awreddy?"

"Yes, Auntie."

"Not enough here for one good name. You buy

one junk name for this, name like Oscar or Blanche, or hard to spell name, Aloysius or Alexandria. Dass all you get for diss."

"Mama-san asks please 'cause the baby no more use the name after one day. They cremate 'um tomorrow."

"Boy or girl?"

"She one girl."

"I give you two names cause your mama-san have hard time. Name the baby Mary Ann. Dass two good names."

As soon as the Naming Lady said "Mary Ann," Melba knew it was right and she suddenly mourned the little sister she would never know. She would never call, "Mary Ann, oh Mary Ann, come for nice prune *mui*." No friends would ever holler from the hibiscus hedge, "Mary Ann can come play?"

The Naming Lady squinted at her, "I name you?"

"Yes, Auntie."

"What I name you?"

"I'm Melba, Auntie, Melba Yamada."

"Melba – dass one high maka-maka name. Dass one of what I call my exclusive names, meaning not so many people have it. I reserve it."

"What my name mean, Auntie?"

"I dunno. I wen get it offa one can peaches."

When one asks a question, they had better be ready for the answer because there are some things it's best not to know. This was clearly one of them.

*

They took baby Mary Ann's ashes to the temple and burned fragrant *osenko* for her little life, while the priest in wide gold robes chanted in mosquito rhythms. At home, three perfect tangerines with their stems and shiny green leaves intact were placed before the framed photograph of Emperor Hirohito. Melba's cousins came on the trolley from Manoa, and Oka-san, numb with grief, fed them. Oto-san had held back some of his catch that morning so they were able to offer the freshest *ahi sashimi* to their relatives, who brought a stalk of ripe bananas and a big bundle of watercress from their farm. Oka-san cooked the watercress in *shoyu* and sugar and served that too, and of course, there was rice, *nori, tsukemono*, and *takuan*.

Melba didn't like Uncle Hideshi, her father's older brother. He was like a pot that bubbles furiously on the stove at the wrong heat. He had such vast cauldrons of rage inside him that it rose in vapors from the top of his head even when he was just innocently sitting in a rattan chair on a nice day. He drank a lot of beer and his silences were towering. When he spoke, it was more a grunt or long rumbling growl than a word. And Auntie

Junko scurried to do his inscrutable bidding. Women always know what their husbands and toddlers want, even when no one else can figure out what on earth they are saying.

Uncle Hideshi grunted for more *sashimi* and Auntie Junko went bowing over with the treasured *Imari* platter. She remained obsequious while he trapped two shimmering slices with his dead-eye *hashi,* and dipped them in the little dish of *shoyu* and *wasabi* in the middle of the platter. Melba found him disgusting the way he held the quivering maroon flesh of the fish in mid-air then gulped it like a greedy dog. As soon as Auntie Junko put the platter back on the table, Oka-san offered it again while everyone else held back, eating mostly *takuan* and rice. Even Oto-san.

The heat of the day was building as the sun moved over the front of the house. Uncle spoke while grunting in piscine pleasure of Japan's glorious victories in Manchuria. Oto-san joined in, rumbling with menace and pride, as if he and Uncle were brother samurai flashing gleaming swords and lopping off Manchurian heads. Melba figured Uncle came to Mary Ann's funeral on the strong possibility of enjoying finest *sashimi* afterwards, and talking about wonderful Japan which could not be so great or he and Oto-san would not have left.

When there was only one slice of raw fish remaining on the *Imari* plate, the Manoa Yamadas got up to leave - or rather, Uncle Hideshi got up to leave and the others followed.

Melba's seven-year-old twin sisters, Hazel and Avis, watched in identical solemnity as Oka-san wrapped a beautiful silvery pink *opakapaka* for the relatives to take home, knowing there would be no fish on their own plates that night.

Melba ran out to her aerie refuge in the arms of the mango tree. From her perch, she watched the Manoa Yamadas walk toward the trolley line. Uncle Hideshi strode out front, swinging his short arms, his oxen legs wide apart as if he needed a diaper change. His three teenage sons, in various imitations, walked behind him: Hideo, Ryozo and Isami. Obviously, Uncle Hideshi had not given money to the Naming Lady so his sons had to make do with un-American names. Auntie Junko, carrying the *opakapaka*, brought up the rear of the family procession, hurrying with short steps, hampered by *geta* and kimono, a silk dragon on her back. Poor Auntie Junko had no daughters to walk last with her.

Melba looked toward the ocean stretching away to where it met the sky and promised herself, "Someday, I will ride the China Clipper. I will fly to far-away places where ladies go first."

33

CHAPTER FOUR

A crisp daughter and meek brother visit a
comatose Melba in the hospital. The daughter
cries crocodile tears. The brother reminds her of
the embarrassing circumstances under which she
acquired the title, "The Mango Queen of
Waikiki."

Suffused with peace, sliced loose from life but
still breathing, Melba floated in a darkness that was
pierced with remembered light. Showers of
incandescence erupted on the periphery of her
awareness, rushing from nothing to nothing the way stars
materialize over the Hawaiian Islands and whole
firmaments sink into morning. It was worthy of
attention. But as soon as she tried to focus on the light
and grasp her situation, it again became a blank screen.
Oblivion.

"Mrs. Matsuda?"

*Where do I go when I'm not here? To what
unknown country deeper than sleep?*

It might have been minutes, maybe hours,
perhaps even days or weeks between thought bursts.

35

I am still me. I'm sure of that. But who is me?
"Mrs. Matsuda."

A voice saying my name. What is the power of my name that it can hold me between light and night, between life and death? What if we knew God's name?

"Mrs. Matsuda? Melba?"

Say it again.

"Mrs. Matsuda?"

Not that name. That's my married name. The other one. Don't you see? A woman surrenders half her power when she surrenders half her name.

Like a battery dying, the names faded. The nurse was busy. Melba moved out of reach, lifted, transported, cells opening into feathers, brain effervescent, blood running in red satin ribbons through old blue veins, tremulous and festive.

I go now with freeway speed, windows wide open, a symphony building to crescendo, to where the road dead-ends. At the last minute, I sprout wings while my vehicle crashes. I am stealing away across dark rivers that whisper to me news of my mother. Far behind are harsh florescent lights, nervous in their beaming. Ahead is a distant light, glowing like the moon with incense before its face.

A new shadow stands before me. I know her well and she is pulling me back, tugging on my freedom as she always has, pulling feathers from my wings, leeching my bones, claiming my red satin ribbons. It is my own flesh, the fruit of my body, given voice and tears.

"Mom," Renee said, staking her claim.

Release me. How can I give you what you need now – or ever? I am a difficult mother, thin and cutting as a blade of grass in my love. I don't mean to be. If you only knew, you might forgive, but truth isn't love, so it won't be enough. You will never have the hugs and smiles I couldn't give when you came in from school, brown and glistening and hungry for my flesh, my soul, my attention. I dreaded your footsteps, the sound of your slippers coming off at the door. Don't cry, Renee. You turn those tears on and off like the kitchen faucet. I'm wise to your ways. Melba felt her daughter's tears dampen her hand, and she raced again into the embrace of darkness.

Surround sound. I need to drown in music. Up the amps. This may be my lucky day, my eternal paradisial Las Vegas. It must be Las Vegas. Where else is there such promise of bliss? See the dazzling, winking lights, the profound sadness of gaiety, the desperation of an entire nation laughing, chinga-chinga, pulling another arm. Yes. My lucky day. Apples and oranges lining up. Next time the pay off. Vast empirical halls of slot machines with a little chair before each one and in each chair a solitary, determined person, one of the most prosperous human beings on the face of the Earth. This may be my lucky day. Each person sitting enthralled, chinga-chinga, lining up apples and oranges, coins tumbling into tin cups, believes himself to be constitutionally entitled to the pursuit of happiness, damn the torpedoes, damn the rest of the world. I believe in America. Full speed ahead. Enlightenment comes in lights bright enough to read by in the middle of the street at midnight. The source of all happiness gushes out of desert arteries, defended by the mightiest army the world has ever assembled. Fill 'er up. Gobble and go. Who guides the guided missiles? Chinga-chinga, me, me. Coffee please, and another trip through the buffet line, all you can eat. Have a cinnamon bun as big as your head, a side of crispy onion rings, macaroni salad, fried chicken, shivering Jell-O, three-bean salad, banana cream pie, Mylanta. I do not want to see those gaunt faces on television, the horrible ribs, the flies partying around pleading eyes, the ancient faces of sick children shining with need. Don't give me a guilt trip. Pass the remote. Switch the channel. Up the volume. Make me happy. Chinga-chinga.

But wait – the sound Melba heard was not chinga-chinga but blip-blip from a machine hooked up to her body, a machine whose payoff was life or death. The biggest gamble.

This may be my lucky day, the day I die. Lucky? Did I say what kind of luck? I'm out the exit. When you leave Vegas, you fly over desert and mountain toward the end of the continent. From the window you look down at the last ragged edge of land where the Pacific rolls upon it with no mercy, and you are overcome with loneliness. You look at that long line of California coast until it is lost under the jet wing as you drone away over the waves with the sky growing dark, heading home. You fly into the uncertain night to small distant islands where the lights have been left on for you and the air is burdened with the sweet, sad smell of flowers.

Vanilla. I smell vanilla. My brother Raymond is here with his orchids. I see him, but not with my eyes. This is curious. He is cradling a ruffled cattleya, an extravagant showy prom queen, the kind he knows I love and which he dismisses as vulgar. He is so tentative and alone, his glasses so thick. He doesn't take up much space on the planet and walks so apologetically across its skin. When did his hair grow so grey? On the internet he buys cymbidiums. Elaine has remarried. She made him choose -- "Me or the prom queens." He chose the orchids and I don't blame him. They are delicate and quiet, and she so opinionated, so disappointed in his tenderness and pension. She destroyed thirty orchids on

the way out the door, blaming them for alienation of
affection, raging against a blush of beauty she can no
longer aspire to, not even surgically. Then she has the
audacity to think she is still entitled to mangoes. She had
the nerve to call me from her new haole husband's
concrete air-conditioned Alhambra in Kahala. "I was
driving through Kaimuki (slumming implied) and I
noticed the mango trees. They're early this year, aren't
they? Well, don't forget your ex-sister-in-law. Ha, ha,
ha."

Melba and her ex-in-law spoke in the musical
cadences of people who have learned they must be polite
to each other because they live on a small island in the
middle of the sea and can't escape each other. They will
never stop running into each other at the mall, a funeral,
Long's Drugs.

"I won't forget."

"When can I come?"

"I'll call you."

They each knew the call would never happen and
sang good-bye, "I'll see you," and hung up without
rancor.

Melba hadn't bothered Raymond with this latest
Elaine mischief.

Raymond put the orchid over on the window
ledge among the other flower baskets where it got lost in

a volume of brassy *anthuriums*, heady ginger, greenery thick enough to support a family of monkeys.

My brother assumes his bloom to be as self-effacing as himself. Why is he so sad when he looks at me? I'd like to smile, Raymond. I'd like to fix your life. I'd like to fix you saimin *and slurp with you like* hana-buttah *days.*

Melba felt herself anchored to the bed when she wanted to alight on his stooped shoulder and laugh in his good ear. She struggled mightily to blink an eye and couldn't. She saw her body as if above it, so pitiful and old, lying as if dead, only a machine registering that a heart still beat inside the prison of slack flesh. And suddenly she was leaving, against her will, drifting again into the ocean of nothingness. Her brother was that last edge of shore about to be lost.

"Oh, Melba," he said, reeling her back in, his love as strong and invisible and non-bio-degradable as *suji* fishing line, the kind that sea turtles choke on.

Then he said no more, so she began to drift again, hearing somewhere that faint music of the stars singing her name in icy plinking notes,

But Raymond once more hauled her in. "Melba, Melba, Melba." He sounded so weary. "I look at you now, and I can't help thinking you have the better part. You don't have to think. What's it like? I would trade places with you if I could. You are the heart of the family, Melba. Without you, we would all drift apart. You call us for Thanksgiving dinner and coordinate the pot luck. Who else will do that, Melba? The kids are too busy. They would do turkey take-out from Zippy's. The twins live in a condo and have no room for the whole gang, and Peter has white rugs and Sachi, and Sachi won't do a pot luck. If you go, Melba, our whole generation falls apart. It's only you. You are the glue, Melba. You don't know how much everyone counts on you. You bring us mangoes. You make the best mango bread. The best, Melba."

Don't keep saying my name. It binds me to this bed of thorns.

As if he weighed a hundred thousand pounds, Raymond sat down in the flatulent brown vinyl armchair beside the bed. He looked everywhere except at her, his eyes gliding over the machine, the flowers, the IV fluids, the urine bag. When he finally ran out of merchandise to examine, he turned his face to her, and tears filled his eyes. "I know you can't hear me, Melba. But I hope that maybe somehow you can feel what I want to say. I feel bad we never say the most important things to the people we love the most. We say how are you, how the kids, been so busy." He dabbed at his eyes with a precisely folded Scottie, adjusted his glasses on his nose, then readjusted them back to where they were. "I want to tell you, Melba, how proud I always was that you were my kid sister. You were so beautiful -- Ka Palapala beauty queen. And you know what, Melba? You are still beautiful. You never lost it. You never walk like one old lady. Your shoulders are so straight and you move with such a quick confidence that I'm jealous. I don't know where you get it. Until this happened, you seemed to get stronger as you got older. That's a fact."

Raymond sat quietly for a long time while Melba rested in her body as if in long grass, contented behind the mask of her immobile face. Then he smiled. "Darren was accepted at Dartmouth. I said I'd help out with room and board. I don't know how I'll do it, but I don't need much. The feeling for your grandchildren is so special, yah?"

Melba wanted to hear more, but she was weary. She felt herself floating. Any second she would be whisked away to the ponderous silence of space.

Raymond heaved himself forward as the chair performed its indelicacies, and he took her hand. They hadn't held hands since childhood. He had a good hand, soft and wide. Unconsciously, his thumb rubbed her knuckles as he spoke. "There were times when I worried about you, Melba. You know, I have a snapshot of you. I bet you wonder whatever happened to it. Well, I'm the one who found it – right on the kitchen floor. Lucky for you, I found it and not Mama. Do you remember the picture? It was when you and Sweetie were hanging out in Waikiki and picking up soldiers. They were crazy – going to Korea and you and your friends went crazy with them." His sigh was most rueful. "But that's all the past. Anyway, I still have the picture. There's something about it, I don't know, I couldn't throw it away. It's the one taken at what looks like the old Edgewater Hotel and you're sitting next to the pool with your feet dangling in the water. You're wearing big pointy sunglasses with rhinestones and you've got two big mangoes stuffed down your bathing suit like *haole* chi-chis. Your mouth is making a kiss. It's really very funny. You look so gorgeous and ridiculous. If it was somebody else's kid sister, I would have laughed, but I couldn't because it was you and there you were with mango chi-chis. I was mad at you. Somebody, probably that soldier Dick Bower, wrote on the back of the picture, 'The Mango Queen of Waikiki.' It wasn't your writing. I thought you would be embarrassed if you knew I saw it, so I just held on to it."

At the sound of that name, Dick Bower, a name unspoken for years, Melba felt a jolt all along her spine. She had forgotten about the snapshot, but not about the tall loose-jointed soldier with eyes as blue as blue ginger telling her, "Blow me a kiss, Honey."

Is that when you stopped talking to me, Raymond, and started grunting at me? When you found that picture? If you only knew what the photograph doesn't show – Dick Bower plucking those mangoes out of my bathing suit and eating them, spitting out the skin, juice drizzling down his arm. Oh, how we laughed. "Wait till they get a load of you back in Indiana, Kiddo." he said. He really loved me. He would have married me. He introduced me to cigarettes and Singapore Slings. I had fun, Raymond. Don't look so sad for me. I never had so much fun in my whole life.

Raymond shook his head. "Remember when you came home Melba? Mama's nose would start twitching the minute you walked in the door. She could smell the cigarette smoke in your hair from fifty yards. She was a human smoke detector. We hadn't had the smell of cigarettes in the house since Papa died."

That was low, Raymond. I am not like Papa. You are annoying me. Stop rubbing my knuckles down to the bone.

As if he heard her thoughts, Raymond gently placed her hand on the sheet and lowered his head, his wrists dangling limply between his knees. "Melba, I've often wondered -- do you ever have any regrets about Dick Bower? Do you ever wonder how your life would have turned out if you married him and moved to Indiana, instead of staying here with Shuzo? Back then, our generation, we didn't ever go against our parents. Mama was too strong for us. But she had to be or we wouldn't have made it without Papa. All these years, Melba, and I have not forgiven our father. I can't. He ruined my life."

Raymond put his head in his hands and began to weep. "He puked on me. He was dead and it bubbled out of him. I've never been able to get the heavy lumpy feel of it off my back. It's still warm, and I'm still surprised. At what age, Melba, does the past lose its grip on us? I'm seventy and I've got that noose around my neck to this day. How do you do it? Tell me your secret."

This is how.

I go away. Like Papa, after all. You see me but I am absent. I am leaving.

But Melba couldn't get escape this time. The darkness did not yawn open before her, nor close around her. She was a stone, not a feather. The shuddering green neon light made her a captive of tubes while she watched her brother cry over his life.

Raymond, Raymond, you're always so discouraged. Don't cling to the downside. Sweep it out of your heart. Bleach the past. But I didn't know about the puke. I'm so glad I didn't. I want to hear about your

happy times. Tell me. Please. We all have choices,
Raymond. The good times or the bad. Which do you want
to hold?

CHAPTER FIVE

A family picnic with curious cousins and scary
stories

At the top of the mountain, at the Nu`uanu Pali
Lookout, where it's so windy the waterfalls blow
upward, Uncle Hideshi parked his truck. It was an
enormous dark green battered vehicle with an open bed
in back, which Uncle fenced in with high posts and slats,
so he could carry his farm produce and chickens to
market. Because of the acquisition of the truck, he
recently expanded his business to include clearing *haole*
and Chinese yards of rubbish and hauling it to the dump.

He had stacks of neatly bundled palm fronds and
panax clippings from the Dolman estate in Nu`uanu
piled high in the back, almost to the top. Eight excited
children sat on the heap, holding it down. Of course,
there was also a burlap blanket weighted with rocks
because children couldn't be counted on to secure all
corners at all times.

The huge old banger clattered and shivered when
Uncle cut the engine. For an instant, silence reigned, and
then the raw wind whirled in with its mighty breath,
hitting the children in grand full force, blowing their hair

in their eyes, swishing under skirts, billowing shirts, inflating egos. They felt such happiness, they were afraid to look directly at each other.

Avis and Hazel began to shriek in high, piercing voices that were swallowed by the derisive wind. Melba was embarrassed for the twins, for her entire gender, while she held down her skirt with both hands.

The cab door opened, and with bassoon grunts, Uncle Hideshi descended, waddled around to the back of the truck and dropped the rear fencing. The boys jumped out first, Raymond and Peter deferring to their cousins, because it was their father and his truck. The boys, without a backward glance, raced to the wall, arms stretched into wings, forgetting momentarily their absurd young masculine dignity.

Oto-san and Uncle Hideshi, also without backward glances, followed their sons, walking in satisfied silence toward the edge of the mountain. Oka-san and Auntie Junko, so pretty in their crisp cotton *yukata*, helping each other, laughing softly, climbed down from the cab where they had been squished between their husbands. Oka-san saw that Melba was out of the truck and helping her sisters, so she too, walked toward the wall, her hand to her mouth to hide her smile. She looked like an angel when the wind caught her wide kimono sleeves. They were two angels, her mother and her aunt, leaning toward each other, whispering and laughing, heads almost touching, black hair, neatly piled, gleaming, coming loose, their feet in pure white tabi and geta, taking small clattering steps.

They were all going on an overnight picnic to clam and fish at Kaneohe Bay. The children each had their own little bamboo fishing poles, nets and pails. The torches were stowed neatly in the corner of the truck bed. The food was on the floor of the cab since the children could not be entirely trusted in this matter either.

Melba ran toward the low lava wall bordering the edge of the cliff, feeling herself almost lifted off her feet by the wind. She was so happy she could almost fly. That's what it takes to fly, she thought, not wings, well, yes, wings, but wings aren't enough. It takes happiness to make you light enough for the wings to work, the kind of happiness that fills your throat with a song beyond words, a spirit song that rises and falls by instinct. That's why birds can fly. It's the song. Wings are just accessories. That's why mynah birds walk around so much. Their songs stink.

Avis and Hazel ran ahead, still shrieking and laughing like stupid girls. They chased each other, long black hair swirling, stinging them like whips.

At the edge of the Pali where it falls off a

thousand feet, Melba paused in awe. She hoped she would never take this sight for granted. Windward Oahu in all its wild splendor stretched out below her: Mokapu humping toward the ocean in sage and tawny mounds, the jagged tooth of Olomana, the parade of sheer green Ko`olau cliffs marching for miles, dividing the island, catching rain clouds, taming the mid-ocean winds so that when they blew over Honolulu they breathed gently. The sea was a hundred hues of blue, capped in white foam, promising immensity and joy, and a horizon that blends with the sky. The air, blowing across thousands of miles of open ocean, was so clean and pure it scoured the lungs and filled them so full of freedom that all things became possible.

Melba knew from history class that this was where King Kamehameha the Great and his conquering army drove the defenders of Oahu, men and women warriors, over the cliffs to their deaths, tumbling into this marvelous air, falling through it, descending to the forest below, so many that their bodies lay in heaps, and Oahu had a new king. It was a magnificent place to die -if you had to die.

Uncle Hideshi clapped. His large hard hands sounded like colliding clouds becoming thunder. Everyone scurried back to the truck. The cousins got in first, securing the best spots, up against the cab.

Raymond and Peter helped their sisters, Peter outside pushing and lifting, Raymond inside pulling the girls up. The cousins watched their skirts fly up even though Raymond did his best to block their view.

The truck coughed into ferocity then started rolling with an admirable show of bluster. It negotiated the hairpin turns on the downhill side of the Pali with a thrilling speed. Hazel and Avis hugged each other, terrified and loving it.

They stopped again, this time at the dump to unload the Dolman's yard rubbish which had served as cushion against the truck's hard metal bed. By the time the children got to He`eia, they were perched just on the cautious side of sullenness. They were appeased by the reckless beauty of the bay, its serene, invasive blueness, the way the green mountains hugged it, and by the importance of this unprecedented family outing.

Reed mats appeared on the grass. On the mats sat at least six different kinds of *sushi*, glass jars of *tsukemono*, big jugs of guava juice, rich little apple bananas, star fruit sliced into precise lemon-yellow stars, and a pot of *nishime,* still warm, brimming with soft carrots, mushy *araimo*, crisp lotus root, slippery *konnyaku*, and dark green seaweed tied in nice knots by Melba early that morning.

The children were allowed to swim. The Manoa

Yamadas stripped to new blue and white *palaka* trunks.
Peter and Raymond wore cut-off pants, Avis and Hazel
were in hand-me-down bathing suits of imprecise origin,
and Melba wore a "dressmaker" suit her mother had
sewn from a flowery remnant. The elastic in the pants
was old so she had to be careful not to lose them when
the suit got wet and heavy. A store-bought bathing suit
would have been the height of richness.

The waters of Kaneohe Bay were tender and
shallow for a long way out, as if the mountains in their
vanity frowned upon the frivolity of surf, and insisted
upon a glassy sea to reflect their own glory. For hours on
end, the children stayed in the water, nudging crabs from
their crannies in the coral, digging clams from the mud,
impatiently waiting for *oama* to bite, passing poles to
one another, going off to play and then returning to
peaceful duty, pole in hand, string dangling, rippling the
water, moving reflected mountains.

On shore, in the fickle shade of the coconut
palms, Oka-san and Auntie Junko sat in their kimonos,
whispering and giggling as they pulled thin aluminum
foil from neat stacks of cigarette wrappers and rolled it
onto large foil balls which would be collected for Japan,
to build airplanes and tanks for victory over China.

When the sun went down behind the Ko`olau,
and the long dark shadows grew deep, the children were

enticed from the sea to dry land by the smell of fresh fish and teriyaki meat sticks on the hibachi. It was still sunny afternoon on the other side of the mountains, in Waikiki, Manoa, Kalihi and Ke`ehi Lagoon. But in Kaneohe the twilight came sooner and the magic of evening got a head start. Shivering and blue-lipped, gangly legs tucked under them, the children settled down to hot green tea and warm food.

Melba thought the sky was the most beautiful sky she had ever seen. She risked saying so. Everyone grew quiet and just looked. The sky lay soft upon the Ko'olau billowing with clouds, pink like a baby blanket. The water of the bay mirrored the colors of the sky, cocooning this far corner of the world in sublime peace. Melba hugged her knees. She was an island unto herself. She needed nothing more than what immediately surrounded her: family, beauty, and food. What else is there?

A canvas was looped over the back of the truck. Everyone would sleep in there except Uncle Hideshi who would have the cab all to himself.

Before they went to bed, while the hibachi fire still glowed, Oto-san lit two oil lamps, making everyone beautiful and dear in the dreamy golden light. The children shifted uneasily in anticipation. The *obake* stories were about to begin, tales of stealth, attack, demon possession, fever, spells and misfortunes, rarely ending in anything but grief and life-long regret. With exaggerated drama, Oto-san rose from the shadows and filled his chest with night air. He grew flushed in the face and gregarious on sake. He pushed back imaginary long sleeves, felt for an imagined sword at his side, screwed his eyebrows into ferocity and began, in Japanese, to tell of Miyamoto Musashi, super-samurai. Shadows stole across him, and his two eyes burned like two coals. He was a handsome, strong father, and Melba loved him so much in that moment that she allowed herself to be led into fear, trusting that when she was sufficiently terrified, he would laugh away the terror – and he did – great thunders of contagious mirth. Everyone laughed with him, and she was so proud of him that joy filled her to the brim. This, she thought as she climbed into the truck to sleep, was the happiest day of her life.

Hazel and Avis, on this special occasion, were generous with their affections and allowed her to curl into their two-some-ness. They were soon warm from collective body heat. Melba smelled old kerosene on the torches, which were kept under the canvas in the truck bed in case of rain, which in Kaneohe could be counted on. In the night, she heard the immaculate rain pass over, moving on toward the mountains, to fill the great lava cisterns with sweet pure water for people to drink.

She slept lightly because she was filled with the
magic of the whole excursion, riding in a truck that
belonged to an actual relative, sleeping in it, so close to
her mother she could more or less accidently roll up
against her and touch inadvertently the soft curve of her
back and buttocks.

She felt her mother stir as her father got up in the
dark. She heard Uncle Hideshi climb out of the cab and
close the door none too softly. The men stole away to
use the public bathroom. The boys awakened each other
with whispers. They gathered up the torches, shaking the
truck as they jumped down. And they, too, were off.

Melba knew it was useless to ask if she could go
torch fishing, because she was a girl and torch fishing
was a male mystery which they kept to themselves. She
climbed from under the sheltering canvas and lowered
herself down into chilly morning and cold dewy grass.
Over the Ko`olau, the vigilant stars hung, spangling the
cloak of night. Out beyond the ocean, the barest hint of
dawn sighed into the sky just above the horizon,
rendering it not as black as black can be.

Men and boys waded into water, not uttering a
word as they scooped up the sleeping *weke*. It must be
nice to be part of something so elementary, so hushed
and ponderous with power and humility. Melba sat on a

rock and watched the torches of the men move away from her, their reflections leaving a burning path in the sea. I want to go, too, and silently carry fire into the morning.

CHAPTER SIX

In which impotent Melba learns of the sexual exploits of the ancient Mr. Lau Yi Ching, and remembers a festive betrothal.

"Morning, Mom." Renee's voice was too loud, too scratchy, too determined to be cheerful, a voice Melba knew well -- Renee had been out partying and whatever time it was now was too early for her to be up.

It wasn't the timbre or volume that summoned Melba back from the amniotic arms of her cerebral holiday, but the need to be alert to clues dropped carelessly like car keys and loose change, clues that might help Melba understand her daughter, or at least know where she spent the night. She couldn't see Renee with her eyes, yet she saw her clearly, from a strange perspective, as if standing on a chair. Renee was smiling and pleased with herself, holding a huge basket of *protea*, their enormous heads stiff and otherworldly on rigid stems. Renee's head, in contrast, was dark, never quite still, chemical curls quivering over her powdered, shadowed face. She looked horribly hopeful. In the vee of her pink blouse, the firm mounds of her surgically enhanced breasts curved in to hints of white lace. It was quite curious, this rather detached appraisal of an unmarried daughter. Melba had heard of out-of-body experiences but didn't think she was having anything so exotic.

I am solidly in my body. I am, in fact, bound and gagged by my body, but why this aerial panorama? It's like being a child again, high in my mango tree, bombs about to fall.

"Look what I brought you, Mom." Renee held aloft the showy flower basket as if she had just won her first soccer trophy. Her surgically altered large eyes made her look perpetually and preternaturally alert. She leaned over and kissed Melba on the forehead. She smelled of too much hair spray, foundation, Shalimar, and breath mints, none of which entirely masked that faint stale whiff Melba always detected when she got too close, a scent reminiscent of the melancholy odor red roses give off as they darken and wilt in the vase.

Melba thought she might like to wipe Renee's face, layer by layer, swab the glop off her eyelashes, rub the fuscia from her lips, erase the false and aggressive facade which took at least thirty minutes a day to achieve. It's what comes of having too much disposable income and no emotional security -- in short, no husband or children though fast approaching forty years of age. Melba, suddenly overwhelmed with tenderness and pity, decided that a daughter with a law degree was as good to brag about as a daughter who produced smart grandchildren.

Renee brushed her hand over her mother's hair, smoothing wisps back from her face, resting her hand on her mother's head in a way that Melba found warm, healing, and slightly uncomfortable. "Oh, poor Mom, you don't deserve this." Renee's voice cracked. She blinked back the tears hovering precariously on the rim of her mascara. Her eyelids were dusted in iridescent blue, silver and lavender, perfectly blended, sparkling like dew. "Don't die on me," she sniffled. "I haven't got it right yet." Abruptly she straightened up, "You're going to be fine, Mom, just fine."

I am not fine. I may not ever be fine. Maybe this is as good as it gets, Renee. If you knew I could hear, you wouldn't patronize me.

Melba wanted to shake her, hug her, and tell her how often she bragged about having a lawyer daughter, but Renee moved away from limp useless arms.

How many times when my arms were quick and sure, did they fail to reach for her as she moved away, reach and grab and draw her shrinking and cringing to my breast and hold her until we were both soft, rounded and comforted beyond embarrassment? It's easy to desire closeness now when it is impossible.

Melba heard water cascading.

"Whoops. I overdid it." At the sink, Renee filled
the *protea* basket with water. "Leaks, leaks. Don't let
anyone move this thing." She settled it on the window
ledge, crowding Raymond's *cattleya* into obscurity, "I
see Uncle Raymond's been here. He's obsessed with his
orchids, isn't he? They're like his kids. He should get a
dog now that he's divorced. You can't curl up with a
cattleya. It won't lick your face." She glanced uneasily at
the ruffled countenance of the bloom. "Or will it? I'm
never sure about these things. Frankly, they give me the
creeps. Maybe they gave Auntie Elaine the creeps, too,
and that's why she left." Renee pulled up a chair to sit
beside the bed. "I don't know if you can hear me, Mom,
but on the chance you can, I'm going to fill you in on all
the latest. They say it's good for coma patients if you
talk to them, that it brings them back. And we sure want
you back – if for nothing else than it's mango season,
and nobody has your mango bread recipe, you old
miser." She took her mother's limp hand.

Melba wanted to correct her, *"It is not mango
season. We may have mangoes but it is not mango
season."* But she couldn't say anything. She couldn't
turn away from the scent of wilted roses. "Mom, squeeze
my hand if you can hear me."

Melba concentrated her formidable will into the

tips of her fingers, imagining messages running along nerves, but not one finger so much as fluttered. Perhaps she could blink her eyes to show she heard and understood. She wasn't sure if her eyes were open or shut to start with.

I cannot blink my eyes. I will take a deep breath. Ask me to take a deep breath, so you can see me respond.

"How's your breathing, Mom? Those tubes must be annoying."

Melba couldn't take a deep breath. *Okay, so there's nothing I can do to show you I am not an eggplant.*

"Do you know what happened, Mom?"

Why does she have to talk so loud? She'll wake the dead. Am I dead? She wouldn't be shouting at me, would she, if I was dead. No, I'm in a bed in the hospital. What hospital? Queens? Kapiolani? Kuakini? Out the window is the state capitol, so it must be Queens.

Melba observed herself looking small and brown and much older than the last time she saw herself in a mirror. Her body was tucked into white sheets in a cold room, in need of a shower and shampoo. She thought she looked like a Martian.

"You fell out of the mango tree yesterday, Mom. Lucky for you, Mr. Resident was passing by. He called

911. He rode in the ambulance with you and stayed in the ER with you until Lance and I got there. That was very nice of him, I thought, considering what a dirty old man he is. I called Cindy in Singapore. She's eight months now and the doctor won't let her fly such a distance, but she calls practically every hour. Kenji was here until about nine last night. He'll be in again this afternoon. I called Auntie Hazel folks and asked her to tell the others. And I left a message on Auntie Sweetie's machine. I didn't say what happened, but I said it was important. I haven't heard back from her yet. She's probably fishing with her *mo'opuna* boys."

Renee placed her mother's hand gently on the white bedding, patted it, then resumed her grip. She laughed, "Mom, do you suppose we'll ever know whether Mr. Lau Yi Ching's last name is Lau or Ching?"

Mr. Lau Yi Ching was from China itself so no one could be sure if his name was really Lau Yi Ching, or whether he still went by the backwards Chinese order of names and was really, in English, Mr. Ching Lau Yi, or maybe Mr. Ching Yi Lau. Melba, somewhat embarrassed at not knowing the name of her neighbor of forty-some years, once asked the mailman, "Which is his last name, Ching, Lau or Yi?"

Lawrence Medeiros had answered, "I dunno. He neveh get no more mail."

"Nutting?"

"He neveh nutting. Ohnee sometime. Da envelope say 'Resident.'" They had laughed, and Melba gave the mailman a loaf of her famous mango bread.

At the supper table that long-ago evening, Melba had recounted her attempt to determine the last name of Mr. Lau Yi Ching. Lance, before he was a policeman with a *haole* wife, while he was still in Kaimuki Intermediate School, said, his mouth full of rice, "Mr. Resident. Dass his name."

His father, dear, dear Shuzo, patiently, always patiently, corrected him, "That's his name. Say your tees. You will be judged by pronouncing your tees. Lazy tees mark a lazy young man. And don't speak with your mouth full. That marks you as a barbarian." Shuzo should have been a teacher. He knew how to admonish without destroying. Melba knew she was a very lucky woman. She thought with shame of the resignation with which she had agreed to marry Shuzo Matsuda, how her mother had turned her bent back and become stone at the mention of Dick Bower and Indiana. In that moment when her life was being decided, Melba had wanted to yell, to yield to hysterics, and finally to be told in anger to go ahead and do as she pleased. But it was her mother's back, unyielding and bent from labor, turned toward her, that had silenced her. Melba could not ask those hunched shoulders to carry one more burden, and so she had married Shuzo, who understood his obligation to have room in his house for a mother-in-law.

Melba now knew that her mother's back was hunched as much from osteoporosis as from the eloquence of hard labor, and that her mother had been right.

Her mother had smiled triumphantly as she watched Melba's fate approaching in the traditional engagement ritual. She and Shuzo's father had arranged it all. The neighbors loved the show as Shuzo's father paraded right down the middle of the street in a long black kimono, holding aloft a huge perfect *opakapaka*, the ritually required red fish. At a small, respectful distance, the *baisha-ku-nin*, the negotiator, carrying the *shugi-bukuro*, the envelope knotted with gold and silver strings and stuffed with money, led the rest of the Matsuda family.

My future mother-in-law was as smug as you, Mama. She looked at me and all she saw was the dutiful daughter-in-law who would be her slave in her old age. Shuzo's two brothers walked stiffly behind her in their dark suits with crisp white shirts and red ties. His three sisters, in starched organdy pinafores, giddy with importance and new clothes, were next. They kept looking over their flounced shoulders to make sure

Shuzo, the star of the little operetta, was right behind them and sticking to the script. They all carried gifts: rice, white hemp, embroidered fabric and *konbu*, the seaweed whose name, when written in *kanji*, also means "child-bearing woman." The neighbors waved, smiled, tossed plumerias.

I watched it all from my bedroom window. I was the only one not smiling. Even in that critical moment I thought of Dick Bower and my dead child. I wanted to run out the back kitchen door while you, with Uncle Hideshi serving as the family patriarch, stood in the parlor sealing the deal. I never did learn how much my life was worth. You took my price to your grave and probably spent it on something for Peter.

Melba came to love Shuzo so strongly, so protectively that when he died – too young at sixty-one – she was shocked at the enormity of her grief. And she became her mother: determined, self-sufficient, while her mother condensed into a fierce shadow in the sunny back room, watching samurai soap operas. Finally, Melba moved her mother to Kuakini Hospital's care facility, where the frail old woman died within the month, by herself, her brow furrowed in anger, her hands coiled in bony spotted fists. Melba felt so guilty and relieved that she had done nothing, said nothing when Avis's daughters swooped in and stripped their grandmother's closet of the best of the old kimonos that had been carried in a sea chest from Japan by a sixteen-year-old girl.

Melba then felt free to sign up for ikebana class, to study the way of tea and go to luncheons and fashion shows of the Japanese-American Women's Club without any sense of capitulation to her mother's insistence on the superiority of all things Japanese. There were no further small or large surrenders to that bent back.

After Shuzo died, Melba faithfully tended his wondrous mango tree, famous as the finest in all of Kaimuki. True, she lost several grafts, but the tree was now bigger, stronger and more productive than ever. And this year, for the first time since Shuzo's lung cancer, a white Pirie mango appeared. It was that mango, or rather, Shuzo would have pointed out, her need to possess it, that had caused her fall.

Renee was asking now, her voice distant and hollow in the uncarpeted hospital room, "How old do you suppose Mr. Resident is? He's got to be in his nineties if he's a day. He's so old he can't get any older. I think certain people in China are born old. I don't think Confucius ever had a childhood – and neither did Mr. Resident.

"Did I ever tell you what Lance and I used to do? No. You'd have skinned us alive. Well, I'll tell you now, and maybe it will shock you out of this coma." Renee shrugged. "Who knows?" She squeezed her mother's hand, "Please come back, Mom. Please. I'm not ready to lose you."

Children hate to see a parent at rest.

Renee's voice fell to a whisper. Melba strained toward it. "Remember the lady way back in the valley who had all the cats? I heard from that cute garage mechanic who had his little illegal shop on the next property, that she had seventy-seven cats and knew them each by name. He said the cat lady went fishing to feed them, and every Wednesday she bought and cooked a turkey for them. One day Lance and I were going into the forest to get mountain apple and we saw Miss Cats all dressed up and going to visit Mr. Resident. At first, we didn't recognize her without her rice-paddy hat and puka pants. She didn't look half bad – in a dress with flowers in her hair. Mr. Resident comes to the door and he's wearing a white shirt and black trousers. Whoa. Now we're really curious. We watched her go in and then we snuck up to the window and what we saw …. Mom, they did everything. Everything. Lance and I couldn't believe it. And when they were finished, Mr. Resident thanked her politely and gave her money. Next thing we see, she's buying turkey for the cats. Lance and I started going to Mr. Resident's yard whenever we could, hoping to see more show. We quickly figured out that Miss Cats went to see him every Tuesday afternoon. So, on Tuesdays, we would hurry home from school and head straight for the old man's yard. We got more of an education there than we did in any health class, let me tell you."

Melba was horrified. That nice Mr. Lau Yi Ching probably consumed so much rhinoceros horn over the years that he personally was responsible for the beast landing on the endangered species list. She wanted to ask Renee how old she had been when her innocence was compromised. Maybe Mr. Lau Yi Ching's appetites had been a terrible inspiration to Renee. Perhaps promiscuity isn't genetic after all; not a legacy of Melba's own brief but exciting reign as the Mango Queen of Waikiki.

Renee seemed to find her memories of the afternoon debauches of the ancients amusing. "I was nine and Lance was eleven. Lance started bringing his friends around for the show and I didn't like that, so I stopped going. I don't know how long Lance kept it up. I think until he got into soccer and they had practice on Tuesdays. Besides, he knew everything there was to know by then."

That filthy Mr. Lau Yi Ching.

"Lucky for you, Mom, that Mr. Resident was

passing by and saw you lying there under the mango tree."

He touched me? That filthy man? Melba tried to remember what she had been wearing, a shortie muu or shorts. One or the other. Why can't I remember? I hope it was shorts.

Renee smiled broadly and answered as if she heard her mother's thoughts, "And lucky you were wearing your ugly long shorts. No can look up, yah, Mom." Abruptly Renee began to talk about Robert Siegel, a client of her law firm.

Melba hated the man although she had never met him.

"Robert Siegel and I went water skiing Sunday. I'm really getting good. You should see me, Mom. One of these days you're going to have to break down and meet Robert. He's really great. You should see his new boat. It looks like a bullet and it's the fastest thing on the lagoon. Those little stinkpot Boston Whalers suck next to it. But it doesn't matter. I know you won't like Robert no matter what. You never like my boyfriends. The only guy you approve of is Glenn Tanaka, good old boring Glenn. Well, Glenn is useful, I'll give you that. He changes light bulbs, swats roaches, paints the bathroom. Every successful woman needs a Glenn Tanaka – a demi-husband on wheels – he comes and goes on call.

Plus, he's Japanese, which for you is everything, huh? He could be a serial killer, as long as he's Japanese. I'm not going to end up like you, Mom, alive, but not living, and I'm not referring to the coma. You always did what you were supposed to do, what you were programmed to do. And what did it get you? Did you ever once, just once, do anything outrageous? No. You were the perfect wife, the good mother, not great but okay, and you were probably the ideal daughter. I'm not anything like you, Mom. Too bad for you." She looked out the window. "And maybe too bad for me."

Melba wanted to cry out. *I was once the Mango Queen of Waikiki.* She wanted to pound her fists against the sheets. *Don't you judge me. You know nothing. Shut up. I don't want to hear your opinion of my life. I don't want to hear about Robert Siegel's bullet boat or Glenn Tanaka painting your bathroom. You're right. You are nothing like me.*

Melba felt tears rise in her eyes, but not enough to spill out. No longer detached and curious about her inert state, she just wanted out. Anger is the great motivator. Where's the exit sign, the fire escape? Where's the window so I can jump?

Renee continued, "Jimmy Ho and I were supposed to go to Vegas next weekend, but of course, I canceled as soon as I heard about you. Jimmy wanted me to go anyway -- 'Look, she's in a coma,' he said, 'Your mother won't know whether you're in Honolulu or Antarctica.' But I said, 'No. I have to be here in case she comes out of it.' So maybe I'm more like you than I thought. I mean, by all rights, I should be packing my sparkles and Spandex and heading for Vegas right this minute." She got up and walked about the room.

"God, I wish you could talk to me, yell at me. Half the fun is gone when you can't get mad. Jimmy Ho knows about Glenn, you know. And you know what? He doesn't care. Of course, he might care about Robert Siegel, if he knew about him, which he doesn't. Robert Siegel would be genuine competition. I'm sure Robert suspects I've got other boyfriends but he doesn't know any particulars, like names. He never asks. He has no right to ask as long as he's living at home with his wife, which is another nail in his coffin as far as you're concerned. Worse yet, he's from Los Angeles, a certified coast *haole* with attitude. And poor nice Glenn – he hasn't got a clue about anybody. He thinks I work so hard at the law library, and that I've always got these depositions and trial preps. God, how can I have respect for anyone that naive? Bank of Hawai'i is lucky he's in their trust department and not in the loan department. If he approved the car loans, everyone on Oahu would be driving BMWs. He wants to take me to Vegas, too, but I can't imagine anything worse than being on the Strip with Glenn Tanaka. He'd probably want to go to the Liberace Museum. Why am I telling you all this stuff? Because, finally I can, I suppose. You have no power over me now. You can't dole out the guilt, so I can afford to be honest. We can't confess to those who have power over us because it gives them more power. But just because I'm suddenly honest with you, don't expect good behavior. Shall I tell you how Jimmy Ho gets all his money?"

Melba began swimming away, frantically. *Jimmy Ho is slimy. I don't want to know how he makes his money.* Confidences of a friend, a brother or sister, the most base confessions, can be handled, assuaged with tea, but a daughter's intimacies cannot be borne.

Finally, she made progress against the current of words, heading for calm waters, leaving Renee behind, smaller and smaller, her voice fainter, more mouse-like, until Melba no longer saw or heard her. The lights were bright behind her but dim ahead -- a long corridor of welcome dusk. She was speeding. Doors opened and closed as she passed. She turned into a passageway on the right, a door swung wide and she entered the freedom of oblivion.

Renee continued to speak to Melba's body. "What am I going to do, Mom? Why am I asking you?

73

You were never any help. I need to ask myself what I really want most in life and what price I'm willing to pay for it. Talking to you in a coma is no different than talking to you not in a coma. You never hear me. Half the things I did, I did so you'd notice me."

CHAPTER SEVEN

Remembering an Infamous Birthday

On Sunday morning, December 7, 1941, Melba awoke with the first downy light seeping through the rice bag curtains, and the first doves cooing in the trees. It was her eleventh birthday. The mynahs were just beginning to rouse themselves into raucous grouchiness, and the palms barely moved as they fingered the edge of the tin roof. She heard her mother moving quietly in the kitchen. The rice was already finished and creamy *miso* soup swelled beneath its lid. Her father would soon be home from his night on the sea, smelling of fish. He'd eat, then go to the bathhouse on Beretania Street and steam until the *mahimahi*, the *ahi*, the *opah* and *kajiki* no longer inhabited his pores.

Melba had slept in her dress so as not to disturb her sleeping sisters. She stepped over them, curled like commas on their futons.

"Ohayo, Oka-san"

Her mother wore a clean navy and white *yukata*, bound by the old maroon *obi* she brought with her from Japan when she was only sixteen. Sticking out from the crisp kimono hem were two knobby, calloused adult feet planted solidly on the immaculate linoleum. Her mother had a bland, nourishing face, not unlike the soup she stirred. Her thick gleaming hair was piled high and anchored by two red wooden *hashi*. She answered Melba's good-morning with a tilt of her head, indicating two absolutely perfect *musubi* sitting on a precisely clipped shiny ti leaf on the table. Inside each rice cake was a tangy pickled plum.

Melba wanted to kiss her mother. She always wanted to kiss her mother, but couldn't. Her family was not the kissing type. They were the bowing type. She scooped up the two *musubi,* knowing they were her mother's kisses.

"Domo, Oka-san." She called her goodbye over her shoulder, "*Itte maeri masu.*"

She was almost out the door when her mother said, with obvious effort, "Happy Birthday," in precise English, the "happy" coming out just fine, the "birthday" a little shaky in the middle.

Melba stopped, so pleased she turned and bowed from the waist, keeping her eyes on the floor. She moved backward toward the door and didn't turn around until one foot was outside. This was the dance they did, she and her mother. The screen door closed and she ran barefoot for the mango tree to wait for Sweetie Waioli.

Every Sunday morning, bright and early, the girls picked plumeria for Sweetie's beautiful mother who danced at La Hula Rhumba on Sunday nights. She paid the girls a nickel apiece to make the leis for herself, the three musicians and two other dancers --sixty-eight flowers exactly for a dancer's leis; shorter, forty-eight flowers for each musician's lei. Plus, there were the hair flowers; 414 flowers in all, 207 each. They had to finish in time for Sweetie to "make nine-thirty Mass" or the nuns would kill her.

Savoring the salty rice flavor of her *musubi*, feeling the crunch of the seaweed wrapper and eating all around the middle, saving the little plum until last, Melba predicted to herself that this birthday would somehow be a day of days. She felt so happy, as if the sun shone inside her body. It was almost unbearable.

She spotted her friend coming along the road running, skipping and walking, swinging her cloth bag, talking to the clouds and trees – not out loud, of course, and not even consciously, just attuned to their harmonies. Sweetie's black hair had a life of its own, springing from her head in quivering wavy abundance. It was Sweetie's eyes, however, that Melba wished to have. They were large, round and brown with a hint of green. They smiled all the time. Melba scrambled down to meet her.

"Hauoli la hanau," Sweetie held out her hand and unclasped a tiny seashell that was the most beautiful

shade of lavender Melba had ever seen. "For happy birthday."

"Where you find dis?"

"Kailua."

"Not."

"For real."

"Try wait." Melba handed her the second musubi then ran back to the mango tree and climbed up. Near the very top hung a small pouch where she kept her treasures. She carefully dropped in the lavender shell and hurried back down.

"Thank you," she said to Sweetie.

"Dass okay. Musubi *ono-licious"* Sweetie licked the last of the rice from her fingers.

Barefoot, they walked and skipped in Sweetie's spontaneous rhythms as they headed into the valley to their favorite trees, the thick ones with low branches. Balancing carefully on wooden planks teetering over gently rushing water, they crossed the *auwai* in three different places to get to the grove just before Mr. Naone's taro patches, where the trees were open to the sun and bloomed profusely, perfuming the air with their soft maternal fragrance.

The girls worked quietly, contentedly, humming and counting as they pinched the soft blossoms from their stems, being careful to take neither buds nor brown-edged "dead heads," and most especially not to break off the clusters for that was not *pono,* righteous.

"Was that seventy-seven or seventy-six?" asked Sweetie.

"Seventy-six. I'm up to eighty-two. Eighty-three, eighty-four..."

Melba heard planes overhead. It struck her that they didn't sound like they usually did. They were not P-40s or Dauntless Dive Bombers, and they were certainly not the China Clipper. Something was off. She continued to pick and count while the planes rumbled on the periphery of her attention. She heard little pops way up high. At first the girls didn't look up. Then they glanced at each other. The noises got louder. The girls stepped from the shade of the plumeria trees, from the umbrella of flowers, and looked to the sky. Planes, like a disturbed swarm of wasps, swooped, soared, darted. Tiny dark puffs of smoke popped into the blue morning sky.

Melba, standing on an old lava wall, shielded her eyes with her arm. "What they doing?"

Sweetie, unperturbed and determined to catch up while her friend was distracted, went back to plucking, "Ninety-two. They must be playing war games or whatevah. Practice for war. Practice makes perfect. Ninety-three ..."

The puffs became dark clouds crowding the sky.

The planes whined and darted. Melba pointed west.
"Look." Thick black smoke towered from the direction
of Aiea and Pearl Harbor. Possibly it was a cane fire, but
not likely on Sunday.

They stood there in the sunshine, flowers in their
arms, faces upturned, and then they saw, as one plane
flew low, the large blood red *Hi No Maru,* the rising sun,
on the underside of the wing. Melba felt her heart stop.
She looked at Sweetie, frightened. "Those are Japonee
planes -- attacking us."

Sweetie bit her lip. "We bettah go for home."

Barefoot, they raced down the valley, skipping
over the *auwai*, planks clattering, flowers flying.
Sweetie's big brother Junior was running to meet them,
eyes wide and feverish with excitement. "It's war. We
having one war. The real McCoy."

Pacing himself to stay behind the girls, he said to
Melba, "I tell your Mama-san I go for you, too. She's so
scared, she crying. 'Wiki-wiki,' she said. I neveh once
heard her say nothing but Japonee."

Melba called over her shoulder, "Sometime she
speak English." She knew it was a flagrant exaggeration
but love and emergency permitted such distortions.

She spotted her mother waiting for her on the
front porch, leaning over the railing, straining to see up
the road. She ran faster, to safety. "Bye," she called as

her friends raced on home.

Her mother hurried Melba inside. The family had gathered around the wooden radio as it broadcast *The Star-Spangled Banner*, "... o'er the land of the free, and the home of the brave." Then the radio went dead. Her father grunted, fiddled with the dials, caught the police band. He had not yet bathed. Peter put his finger to his lips. Melba was making too much noise with her short breathing. Raymond grabbed her hand. Hazel and Avis looked at her solemnly, still in their nightshirts. Their fishy father kept his ear to the radio and appeared not to notice her arrival, had perhaps not noticed her absence or considered her jeopardy, being out there, unprotected under the open sky, away from home while bombs fell. He was pale and silent. Melba realized that Oto-san, the invincible samurai father, was frightened. She wanted to cry. Tears spilled over. No one noticed except Raymond, who squeezed her hand. He was her favorite. She was his favorite.

The radio bristled with static and urgency. Anyone with medical training was asked to report to Pearl Harbor at once. Citizens were ordered to stay off the streets. Flames and thick black smoke rose from Pearl Harbor. Burning ships succumbed to the sea. Schofield Barracks has been strafed, the airfield at Hickam destroyed. Closer to home, the tofu factory on

Kukui Street had been hit. Someone needed an ambulance on McCully Street.

Except for the radio, it was so quiet inside the Yamada house, it was like someone had been born or died.

The attack lasted two hours. By the time the last red-emblazoned wings peeled away from Oahu, Pearl Harbor, Wheeler, Hickham and Kanehoe Marine base all lay in ruins and more than three thousand people were dead.

The Yamada children went out in the yard and sat under the mango tree. They knew their parents needed to be alone to speak in whispers of Japanese. Hazel asked, "Why the Japonese bomb us? Don't they know we Japonee, too?"

Peter snapped at her from the full gangly majesty of his fifteen years, "We're not Japanese. We're American. Don't say we're Japanese, 'cause we're not."

Avis, who could be annoyingly precise, said, "We both."

Raymond, always the mediator, offered, "Our parents are Japonee because they born in Japan. We American 'cause we born on American soil, but because our parents are Japonee, we're li-dat too, but not really. It depends on where you born."

Peter grew angrier by the second, losing the

haole-sounding English they drilled into him at Roosevelt High School, "If you say you one Japonee, that means you the enemy. Our country is at war with Japan now. The Japanese attack us. They coulda killed us. To them we're not Japonee, we're American."

Hazel asked, "Are Oka-san and Oto-san the enemy?"

Everyone looked to Peter. He threw a handful of dirt. "They're just our parents. They're nothing to nobody else."

"Anybody else." Melba corrected him. She liked his *haole* English. She planned on speaking it, too, when she got to Roosevelt High School. She always paid careful attention to the radio announcers, and she practiced when alone in the high branches of the mango tree.

Peter threw another handful of dirt. "I wish I was older. I'd fight for my country."

Melba suddenly felt sick to her stomach. She ran to the hibiscus bushes, hand over her mouth. With great satisfaction, she threw up, heaving and gasping, then sat down in the grass. On her eleventh birthday, her life, her whole world, changed forever.

Peter sat beside her, putting his hand on her forehead. "Are you okay?"

She nodded, her eyes tearing from the strain of

vomiting. "I'm empty."

Avis and Hazel brought their mother, who fussed over Melba and led her to the house, easing her down to the bedroom futons which, in all the commotion, hadn't yet been folded up. Oka-san washed Melba's face with a cool cloth, put a glass of water to her lips and soothed her with soft Japanese words.

CHAPTER EIGHT

In which a single teardrop leaves a trail on an ashen cheek.

The twins, chubby and buxom, perched around Melba's hospital bed, conversing and flapping about like mynah birds, fussing, scolding each other, so self-important and ridiculous with hair too bouffant for the times, that Melba wondered how they did it, how they were so jointly out of step. Did they consult each other and agree to the poufs and pants? Or was their identical bad taste part of the mysterious twin force?

What is that poem -- Don Blanding – some snippet that says mynahs are mankind's in-laws? Well, they are also womankind's sisters.

Hazel, the more fatalistic of the two, feasted on disease, car wrecks and sacrificial relationships. She asked Avis, "Did you always ever wonder who would be the first of us to go?"

Indignant, Melba wished to protest. *I'm not dead yet.* She would have settled for a withering glance, but she couldn't even muster that.

Avis answered, "No. I leave that to you. Death, divorce and disaster are your department. Mine is money. I used to wonder who would be the first of us to make a million."

Hazel's voice had a dreamy, far-off quality, "I always just assumed it would be Peter. He's the oldest."

"To die or make a million?"

"Die, of course. It would be the natural order for him to go first. We're the youngest. We'll be last."

Melba wished to enter the fray. *Don't count your chickens, Sister. Life changes in an instant. In a twinkling. Nothing is secure. No one is safe. Everything is in motion -- except me. I'm a stone.*

Avis rolled her eyes theatrically. "Peter is above the natural order and he's already made his million. He beat me to it, that's for sure." She fussed with a jade and sapphire pendant. "He made so much on that waterfront development that he can -- and did -- buy the natural order."

Hazel laughed lightly, a little meanly, "Yeah, like his face lift."

"You think he has?"

"I know he has. Do you know how many faces a day I see at the Elizabeth Arden counter? I make them up, make them over. Everyone wants to look young, thank God for me since I work on commission. Trust me, our brother has had a face lift."

This was new information for Melba. She never

thought of Peter as "cheating."

Hazel sighed deeply as she looked down at Melba. "Our poor sister would not want to be a vegetable. She wouldn't want to live like this. I wonder, does she have a living will? An organ donor card?"

Melba panicked. She imagined them scooping out her eyeballs, her kidneys while she was as alert and powerless as she was now.

Avis looked around the room. "Renee would know. Knowing Melba, Little Miss Goody-goody, she'd want to donate her kidneys and eyes to help other people."

Yes, but not while I'm still here, you idiots. A kidney is not a mango.

"It's too soon to talk about pulling the plug," Hazel said, infuriating Melba further. She ran her hand across Melba's forehead. "I should put some moisturizer on her. Her skin is so dry. You know, I never thought Melba would be the first to have something really bad happen to her. She was always the strong one. I always get the feeling that if something happens to Melba the whole family falls apart. Melba – you there?" She shook the bed.

"Don't do that."

"Why?" Hazel shook it again, "Anybody home? Melba. Oh, Melba."

The way you're shaking the bed, Sister, you'll scramble my remaining brains.

In the presence of her sisters, Melba felt truly helpless, defeated. She couldn't rise up and strangle them or wither them with words. *I will never speak to them again and they will not get a mango or a kidney as long as I live. Live? Look at me, imprisoned in this bed. I might as well be dead.*

Hazel turned smugly to Avis, "See -- she's not there. If we don't pull the plug, who's going to take care of her? I have a job. Renee is useless, Cindy's in Singapore and that daughter-in-law is *haole* –she'll feed our sister mashed potatoes."

"Don't look at me. I work harder than you. I've got my real estate and my earrings. Besides, Renee can marry Jimmy Ho, unless he gets arrested, and be rich and have a big house on Hawai'i Loa Ridge and hire a nurse to take care of her poor mother." Avis smiled. "Besides, Melba won't fit in my Porsche with a wheelchair, so how can I help?

Avis drove a silver Porsche, Hazel a silver Mazda which she thought of as better than a Porsche, although she was acutely aware that no one else did. She loved hearing about Avis's repair bills. She derived her own satisfaction from parsimony and good parenting, qualities she found lacking in her twin. She said, "Well,

I'd somehow make room for her in my car. I'd even sell it and get a van if I had to."

"I'd sell a Mazda in a minute, too."

Melba wearied of them. Her eyeballs ached. *We spoiled the twins. We always spoiled them. They're so selfish.*

Hazel, to regain the upper hand, asked Avis, "So how are your kids?"

"Don't ask. Ask – so how's your business?"

"Okay – so how's your business?"

"Great. I've got these Hollywood clients -- one of them used to be married to Julia Roberts' ex-husband's cousin. They're interested in the Dillingham estate in Hana. If I can put the deal together, I can quit making those stupid earrings."

"Maybe Peter can help you."

"Peter? Pff. He still treats me like I'm his baby sister, when I'm old enough to get senior citizen discount at Daiei."

The twins didn't notice Raymond walk into the room, slouched and self-contained. He looked worried and dull beside their bouffant effervescence. Melba felt that his arrival saved her life.

"Hi," he said, tentatively. He looked at the twins through his coke-bottle glasses. "You should be happy someone treats you like a baby anything at sixty-four."

Avis asked, "How can you defend Peter? I bet he still treats you like the tag-along little brother."

Almost in a whisper, Raymond said, "My brother treats me like a stranger."

Hazel shook her head. "It's nothing personal."

"That's what I said. It's not personal."

They all laughed in varying degrees of humor and resignation.

Avis said, "Peter's not bad. He's just afraid of us. He's afraid we might need something."

Hazel said, "I blame his wife."

"Which one?"

"I don't know. They're all alike. Mona, Tessa, Sachi. They just keep getting younger."

"Sachi is a sharp dresser."

"Who wouldn't be? If I had her money …."

Avis corrected her, "She has Peter's money."

"Whatever money. I'd look like, like Cher."

Avis sniffed, "You would."

Raymond changed the subject, "So, Avis, how's the old taro patch?"

"Don't mention it. I can't believe a daughter of mine lives down in Waipio Valley without electricity, up to her elbows in taro muck and so happy I could spit. Ask me about my business, then I'll have good news."

"Don't ask her, Raymond," Hazel begged.

"Please. I can't stand it."

Can't they see Raymond wants someone to ask him about his grandchildren? Darren just got accepted at Dartmouth. Ask him, you self-centered idiots – one of you. Please. Melba surprised herself by remembering Dartmouth, a fact acquired while lying in the hospital. Of course, nobody noticed. Who pays attention to a vegetable?

Raymond inquired of Hazel, "Hear from Cheryl and the grandkids?"

See? He's dying for you to ask him about his grandchildren. Ask.

Hazel launched into a litany of her grandchildren's achievements in various levels of school, sports, and clever discourse. They lived in Los Angeles.

Avis interrupted and slyly asked what shade of lipstick she was wearing.

"Mozambique."

The conversation floundered at that point, and suddenly Peter was in the room, his cologne announcing him. He nodded at Raymond, and put his arms around the twins before turning his attention to Melba. "Hey, little sister, we're counting on you. You're going to be fine. You'll see. You just have to hang in there. You're a toughie." He checked his watch and turned to the other siblings, "Where are her kids?"

"Who knows?"

"Did my flowers arrive?"

"You mean that jungle over there?"

The huge bouquet of *anthurium*, bird of paradise, ginger and miscellaneous tropical flora took up an entire table. Peter walked over, read the card. It was his. "I've got to run." He went to the head of the bed, bent and kissed Melba on the forehead, his lips not quite touching her skin.

She sensed his terror.

He hurried away without a backward glance.

Avis said, "That was fast. Was he really here? Or did we imagine it?"

Hazel answered, "At least he came."

The twins fell to discussing the men in their ballroom dancing class, laughing about toupees and the timidity of the recently widowed. They were both divorced, Avis twice, not counting a three-year live-in that ended with a restraining order. Simultaneously, without signal, they both got up to leave. They kissed Melba on the forehead, one from each side of the bed, smothering her in identical storms of Blue Grass perfume. Squawking and laughing, they flitted away into the corridor, arm in arm.

With profound relief, Melba settled into the calm

lake of their absence, Raymond beside her.

He took her hand. "I'm so proud of Darren. I told you yesterday that he got admitted to Dartmouth. And he got a partial scholarship. I'm going to help out a little. I wish I could do more. Melba, did I ever tell you how much you mean to me? After Papa died, you were the only one who believed in me. You always thought I was so clever and you called my small achievements to Mama's attention. You were the rock of the family, Melba. Not that Mama wasn't strong or didn't love us. But she always worked so hard she was too tired for anything but putting food on the table. And she and Peter had their pact. Everything for Peter. I give you the education, and you take care of me. She practiced triage in the family. And Peter got off easy – you took Mama – she lived with you until she went to Kuakini. Do I sound bitter? I hope not. I wish him well. I just don't care to be around him. We have nothing in common except that we lived under the same roof in hana-buttah days."

A tear rolled down Melba's cheek. She felt it, wet, trailing. She was as astounded by it as Raymond.

He shouted, "Nurse! Nurse!" No one came. He rushed into the hallway, still looking back at Melba with the damp snail of tear on her dry skin, afraid to take his eyes off her. He continued to shout until a nurse hurried toward him. "I'm sorry to make such a commotion, but my sister cried. A tear came out of her eye."

The nurse calmly checked Melba's pulse, her machines and dials. Melba wanted to cry out in ecstasy: *I'm here*!

Finally, the nurse said, "This is not necessarily a sign of cognition. Tearing is an involuntary act." With a professional surety, she lifted Melba's eyelids and beamed a small flashlight in one eye and then the other. The light hurt. "We just don't know with these things. I'd say it might be positive. But it may mean absolutely nothing. People get excited if a finger moves, but usually it's just muscle spasm."

I'm here, you idiot. You'll never get my mangoes or kidneys.

When the nurse left, Raymond grabbed Melba's hand. "I know you're there, Melba. I'll stay with you awhile and talk about little-kid times. And you'll come back all the way when you're ready. And I'll bake mango bread for you with your own mangoes. It won't be as good as your bread, but you never shared that recipe. Shame on you, Melba. Now see -- you'll have to eat mine. I put coconut in it trying to make it as moist as yours, but it's never the same."

Flow eyes, flow. Let them know. No more tears came, but Melba's excitement and happiness grew. *I will share my recipe when I get out of here. I do not wish to*

waste calories on inferior mango bread, so save yours.
Send it to Darren at Dartmouth.

CHAPTER NINE

In which Emperor Hirohito suffers an indignity and the children of Hawaii are fitted with gas masks.

      A breeze soft as fingertips on skin whispered down Kalihi Valley, barely stirring the palms on its way to the open sea. Melba sat sideways on the porch steps, her back against the pocked lava rock, reading her American history book. She glanced up from The Gettysburg Address - which she loves - to see a car slowly coming down the street. It paused, then parked by the hibiscus hedge. Two *haoles* in suits got out. She closed her book, then stood, clutching it to her chest, as if Abraham Lincoln could shield her.

      The men sauntered into her yard with the authority of landlords. One had a bony head too small for his shoulders and teeth too big for his mouth. The other had a stomach so fat his jacket buttons looked as if they'd pop if he burped. The toothy one spoke, "Your papa-san home, Kid?" His voice was friendly and false like Leo Chang's before he punched you in the stomach in the playground.

Melba pulled Abraham Lincoln closer and shook her head no.

The men walked right past her and up the steps. Peter came to the screen door but didn't open it. In Lord-Fauntleroy English that made Melba want to laugh in her nervousness, he asked, "Excuse me, gentlemen, but who is looking for our father?"

The toothy one pulled a small black leather folder from inside his jacket and showed Peter a badge. The one with the stomach, out of breath from four steps, mopped his forehead. "F.B.I. Now where's your old man?"

"Our parents are not at home."

Melba detected a slight crack in Peter's voice, which might have been fear, or just a symptom of his age. She couldn't tell.

The men opened the screen door and brushed Peter aside with their suited shoulders as they walked right in the house, leaving their shoes on, the fat one muttering, "You can't trust a Nip. Not even a young one. They lie through their eye-teeth."

Melba caught the screen door before it closed, and slipped behind her brother, like a shadow.

The toothy one, scanning the tiny white room said, "They can't help being sneaks. It's in their blood."

Raymond stood by the closed door of the girls'

bedroom. The men glanced at each other and took guns from their jackets. Melba felt the breath go out of her. She had never seen an actual gun. Something cold and sinister had entered her little house and the house seemed to crouch in its presence.

The toothy one motioned to Raymond with his gun, "Outta the way, Punk."

The crack in Raymond's voice was now definitely fear, so his refusal was all the more remarkable. "Please. It's just my little sisters in there. They be scared."

The stomach one said, "Yeah sure. Your old man's in there pissing his pants." He shoved Raymond out of the way. Both men aimed their guns at the closed door. "Come out with your hands up."

Melba began to cry. No one noticed.

Peter stepped in front of the guns, "There are only two little girls in there. Let me open the door and you can see for yourselves."

The men moved to either side of the door, nodded, and cocked their guns. The toothy one said, "Go ahead, Wisenheimer. Open."

Peter turned the knob. The click was loud as a disapproving tongue, the hinge creaked. Hazel and Avis were sitting in a corner hugging each other, their twin faces pressed next to each other, eyes as wide as open flowers.

In a voice as heavy and triumphant as Oto-san's samurai impersonations, Peter taunted, "Happy? There's the great yellow peril."

The toothy one grabbed Peter by his t-shirt and put the gun to the side of his head, "Don't wise off, Kid. There's martial law in effect and I can get a medal for blowing your Jap brains out."

"Hey," the stomach one said, "They got a radio."

"Your old man sending congratulations to Tojo?" The toothy one yanked Peter's shirt again.

The other slipped his gun back in its holster, kicked the radio from the table, ripped out the insides and smashed them. Then he noticed the faded picture of Emperor Hirohito on the wall. "Ah so," he said scornfully, as if he had found a cache of arms. "The honorable emperor himself."

The toothy one still had his gun out. He jabbed Peter with it, "What would you do, Nip Punk, if your Emperor came to Hanalula?"

"He's not my emperor. I'm an American. Just like you."

"Oh yeah? Well, you don't look like an American to me. Take the emperor down."

Slowly Peter walked to the wall, reached, struggled a moment with the wire, then turned to hand the photograph to the fat one.

He pulled back, "I ain't touchin that thing. Throw it on the floor."

With both hands, Peter raised the picture. He glared at the toothy man with the gun, and then with all his might, he threw the emperor to the floor. Glass flew everywhere.

"Step on his face."

Peter ground his bare heel into the paper, leaving a thin thread of blood from the glass in his foot. He kept his eyes on the man with the gun.

The toothy man put the gun away, "You tell your old man come see us." He took a card from his wallet. When Peter made no move to accept it, he threw it on the floor. "Tell him bring his papers and the papers for his boat or we'll come back and arrest him and send the lot of you back to Tokyo where you belong. Got it?"

They left, sauntering away as arrogantly as they had arrived. The twins began to wail and rushed across the glass to Melba. She couldn't help it, she cried, too. Even Peter had tears in his eyes, but his were a different kind. His chin was rigid, his fists closed. He walked out of the house, making a thin trail of blood on the linoleum floor. Through the screen door, Melba watched him lean against the mango tree, his head against his arm.

Raymond lifted Hazel from Melba's embrace and

carried her across the glass to the bedroom, came back for Avis, then got the broom. "Tell em a story. Check their feet. I clean up."

Melba retrieved her history book from the floor. She read them the Gettysburg Address. She got as far as, "all men are created equal," and she could go no further. She closed the book and began to tell the twins the love story of the slender maiden Green Willow and the samurai Tomodata. They sighed deeply, first one, then the other. They knew the story well. They loved Green Willow.

*

The next afternoon, Melba, with Sweetie right behind her, climbed high into the mango tree, which of course had no mangoes in December, so they were eating tough *jabon*. Sweetie's long wavy black hair fell about her shoulders. Her eyes were stars, solemn and bright with mischief as she spoke. "Helen Takahashi just walking down Smith Street got her arm blown off." She peeled more thick yellow skin from the fruit, tore off another segment and jammed it in her mouth while the skin tumbled down through the leaves of the mango tree. Sweetie would, someday soon, be as beautiful as her mother. She had the same feline poise and she moved with the same insouciant grace.

It was difficult to top Helen Takahashi's blown-

101

off arm but Melba needed to deliver worse news, without revealing the ultimate worst news, the scene she could hardly bear to think about. She offered instead, "McCully Street one whole block burn down."

"Yeah. Lunalilo School, too. Too bad our school no get hit."

"Yeah. Tomorrow, we go back." Melba paused to spit a pit. "One good ting -- no more Japonee language school after school. The army close Hongwanji mission and take away the priests."

"Not!"

"Yeah."

"The priests?"

"Um hum." Melba waited, her abundance of calamity mixing carelessly on her lips with the *jabon*'s bitter juice, then said, "One bomb land right in Waikiki."

Sweetie, realizing she has fallen one disaster behind, breathlessly related, "The Goos got 'em one bomb right in a house."

Melba finished chewing some *jabon*, spit more pits, then delivered news that was very close to the news that caused her to blush with shame. Very quietly, with as much detachment as she could summon, she said, "American planes shot some fishermen out in a sampan. The Coast Guard towed a boats in, and da families wen go down and getta bodies. Oto-san know dem. He real mad, curse like crazy."

"What he say?"

"I dunno. We no learn those Japonee words at Hongwanji mission."

Sweetie was suitably impressed, "Lucky for you your papa-san awready back that day."

"Lucky he awready had plenny fish."

"They arresting Japonee people, you know." Sweetie's eyes widened with urgency. "Take 'em to Sand Island. I ask my mama. She say you can stay wid us if your folks get arrested."

"I scared, Sweetie." Melba looked at her friend and was betrayed by tears, big tears that squirted from her eyes as words tumbled from her mouth. She was unable to dam up either. "The F.B.I. come to our house. They mess it all up, look everywhere. Oto-san and Oka-san not home. They take one gun and hold it right at Peter's head. Li`dis." Melba put her finger to her temple. Her hand trembled.

Sweetie's voice was hushed and respectful before the enormity of a gun being put to the head of someone she knew personally. "Not."

"They tell Peter take da picture of Emperor Hirohito an dey make him trow it on a floor and smash it wid his foot. The F.B.I. tell Peter tell your faddah come see us and bring his papers, or we come back an arrest him and send da ho family at Tokyo.'"

Sweetie stopped peeling *jabon*. The leaves of the
tree whispered in the tradewinds. "You tink they come
back?"

"I dunno. I tink Oto-san scared. He tell Oka-san
he no have no more papers. He come illegal alien." She
sniffled. "I scared the F.B.I. come back. I scared the
Japonees come back."

"You tink the Japonees come back?"

Melba abruptly stopped crying. Rescued by
sudden and surprising anger, she glared at her friend.
"How should I know? I'm not Japonee. I born here. Just
like you." Abashed at herself, she immediately retreated
to concentrate on the unyielding skin of the *jabon*.
Digging in with her fingernails, she felt the little citrus
mist spring up to her nose.

Into the silence, Sweetie said quietly, tentatively,
"Junior signed up for the army awready."

Her mouth full of *jabon*, Melba answered, "Peter
says he wish he can go, but he no more old enough."
The friendship was back on solid footing.

"Junior say if the Japonees come back now, they
just take us. We no more boats, we no more planes, we
no more nutting. All a sailors dead. He saw da coffins
stacked up on King Street."

"Oka-san make us each one little bag. If we need

to go *mauka*, to the forest, we take extra clothes and food in em."

Sweetie was thrilled. "Your mama-san make one bag for me?"

"She too busy. She working to help Matsufuji-san clean a tofu factory so she get her job back. But we can make em ourselves."

The door to Melba's house opened. She quickly put her finger to her pursed mouth. She was not supposed to be up in the mango tree.

The girls' eyes were merry as they bit their lips and scrunched their shoulders.

Melba's father kicked a tin bucket off the steps and ran his hand through his thick uncombed hair. He leaned against the door jamb like a flower too long in the vase, his head too heavy for his neck. Then he saw something – the fresh yellow *jabon* peels on the ground under the tree. With a samurai roar he charged the tree, grabbing the trunk, bellowing in Japanese for Melba to come down or he'll shake her down this minute.

The girls scrambled to the ground. Melba smelled sake on her father's breath as he continued to yell. Sweetie ran home. Melba meekly went in the house, head lowered, steps small, showing no panic. She felt her father's oaths scorching her back even though he had not yet come in the house. She carefully measured out rice from the big tin cannister and began to wash it, saving the first rinse water for the garden. If she kept busy, her father would be satisfied. The military had closed Honolulu harbor. No boats could go out to sea except military boats. Her father had been afraid to go to his sampan since the other fishermen were shot and he, himself wanted by the F.B.I. He had finished mending his nets. Without his boat, he had nothing more to do.

When her mother came home from the tofu factory, exhausted, her kimono and coiled black hair dusted with flour, Melba had the rice cooked, ginger grated, and green onion sliced. Oka-san produced two eggplants. She was like magic.

After supper, her mother, with a gravity that was almost ceremonial, gave Melba money. She told her to go to the Ritz Department Store on Fort Street after school the next day, and buy her an American dress. Melba tried to picture her mother in an American dress, but she could not.

*

At school, soldiers came and issued gas masks to all the children, telling them they had to carry them at all times. They paraded the children out on the lawn then showed them how to put the masks on and use them. Melba lifted the horrible mask toward her face. It smelled acrid and rubbery. Everyone looked like monster bugs. Some boys jumped around executing karate chops in the air, doing their best to be frightening. Most were nervous, dropping the masks and trying again. Some girls cried. The criers got a lot of attention and Melba wished to be frightened enough to cry. Tears always come at the wrong time. When you want them, they're dry as an old *lauhala* hat. She was too excited to cry. The preservation of her life was, after all, important enough to merit a gas mask from the United States government. At least all children are created equal.

With their new masks over their faces, the children were ushered to a classroom filled with tear gas. This time, Melba cried. Her eyes felt as if they were being cooked on the hibachi. A soldier led her outside, fitted her with a new mask, then motioned her back into the gassed room. She shook her head in protest, so terrified she thought she might wet herself. The soldier gently led her back inside. She closed her eyes, held her breath, felt dizzy. He patted her on the back, forcing her to exhale and take a new breath. She opened her eyes. His were smiling behind his mask. He bent down, looked directly at her, then gave her the thumbs-up okay sign. This mask fit.

She returned to her classroom, red-eyed and happy, the object of much attention. Mrs. Lane took her to the girls' lavatory and helped her wash her face and rinse her eyes. "There now. Feel better?" The teacher smelled like talcum powder and perspiration, the reassuring scent of benign female authority.

*

The bulky gas mask and its clumsy canvas pouch kept getting tangled in the racks of clothing as Melba wandered through the crowded aisles of the Ritz Department Store. It was her first time in the Ritz. There was so much to buy. Who had such money? She found herself in the mysterious and fascinating world of women's lingerie -- brassieres, panties, slips, camisoles, nightgowns. On a rack against the far wall, she saw what appeared to be nice flowery dresses in baby blue, pale yellow, pink and lavender. The sign read, "Just Arrived. House Coats." The sign was slightly yellow on the edges. House coat. That must be what American ladies call dresses. Melba had never heard the term before, but she liked its formality. It sounded suitable for a first American dress for one's mother. She chose the lavender. It was loose, more or less tent shaped, and had a little violet bow by each buttonhole. It was very pretty.

The saleswoman assured her she had made a good choice, *"Cairina, ne?"* She folded the garment in precise origami lines, wrapped it generously in two layers of tissue paper, put it in a bag and presented it to Melba, bowing as she held it out. Melba accepted the parcel and returned the courtesy, feeling very important.

When her mother came home that evening, she unwrapped the American dress, held it up, nodded her approval for almost a full minute, and then with a weary sigh let it fall back into its tissue.

In the morning, when Melba got up, Oka-san was in the kitchen wearing the crisp new lavender house coat. She smiled at Melba. She had cut her black hair short and curled it. She was a stranger. She wanted to be called Mama.

CHAPTER TEN

The old war hero visits The Mango Queen in the hospital. He tells her about rosy-cheeked Germans and the ghost people of Dachau.

"I dunno, Melba. I always thought you would be the one taking care of me. I'm on six kinds of medication. My heart can go any minute, but I keep fooling the doctors. I never give up my *shoyu* and the thing still ticking." Kenji seemed genuinely puzzled by his continued existence. His height and his baby-smooth skin deceived even himself into an illusion of health.

In a rush of uncharacteristic tenderness Melba wanted to reach out from her bed and take his hand in hers, but she was still in the soft summertime of helplessness, drifting like golden pollen and seed-down on the surface of green grass, alighting and lifting, gossamer, ephemeral, borne away. Maybe drugs were like that. Maybe that was the appeal, this lassitude that is bliss, this suspension from the tyranny of time. This safe place. Suddenly a terrible thought pierced her: A person does not easily surrender such a refuge. Just for a moment, she understood Renee, and then wasn't sure what it was she had glimpsed so clearly.

Kenji went to the foot of the bed and lifted the blankets. He took her right foot in both his age-soft hands and began to massage it, starting at the ankle, working slowly down the heel and along the instep, using his stout thumb on the bottom while his other hand softly caressed the top. He moved to the ball of her foot, and finally her toes, working each toe individually from the stem to the head, then squeezing them all together. He repeated this with her left foot, taking his time, talking in his slow easy way.

"You think Melba, I don't want to get married because I don't want to mess up our social security or pensions and because we need to make sure our property pass each to our own kids, and that's true, but that's not all of it. I think Melba, I don't want to marry you because I'm afraid. I already lost too much. When Yoko passed away, I promised myself I would never remarry because I never want to hurt that bad again. It's like when I put Kimo to sleep. Remember the day? I was so broke up I promised myself I would never get another dog. You understood. Well, it's like that -- no insult – Kimo was the best. I guess what I'm trying to say is I didn't know I loved you so much until this happened. So, after all, there is no protection from love. It gets down to two things, neither of them good. Either you lose the person you love because they die or divorce you, or you get saved from that pain by leaving or dying first. Either way, Melba, I hurt so much I think I might as well marry you."

Melba wanted to sit bolt upright in bed and say, *"Kenji, you are about as romantic as a jellyfish. You think I can't hear you because you think I'm half dead. And furthermore, what makes you think I want to marry you anyway? Oh, I did when I first met you. I wanted to replace Shuzo. I didn't know any life but married life. But you know what? I have come to like our arrangement. You live in your place. I live in mine. I don't have to clean up after you. I have my whole bed to myself and it smells like Avon body lotion. You come and take me to dinner at Wisteria and McCully Chop Suey and to Four-Four-Two parties. Sometimes you stay over. What more can I want?"*

But she couldn't do anything except lie there and be proposed at. She wanted to fly away unbound, change shape, but Kenji kept saying her name, holding her by its many tangled strings, and she couldn't escape.

He droned on, "But there's something you need to know about me first, Melba, and then you might not want to be part of what I am. You see, I never told anybody about the war, but I think of it every day. Not a day goes by. It's as much a part of me as my skin or my lungs. It sits in my mind patiently waiting for a moment of fatigue or weakness. It has eyes. It watches. It wants to grow. So, I keep it locked up. But it's like not telling you my real name, like maybe not even knowing my real name, yet knowing that Kenji, the guy you see, is an imposter." His hands continued their loving work, massaging as he spoke in a tone like distant thunder leisurely coming over the ocean, taking its time. "We went through battle after bloody battle. So many Hawai'i boys died in the cold with no leaves on the trees, so far from green mountains. All the time we're driving the Germans back, all the time back. I think the people in the German towns had never seen an Oriental before. They thought they were the master race and here's some slant-eyed Japs in American uniforms marching into their towns and taking over. They were very quiet and sullen. I remember they had rosy cheeks and hostile blue eyes.

"This one town we came to was different. It makes my hair stand up to this day -- *obake* chicken skin. We moved through, street by street, and no one would look at us. It was like they felt a mix of shame and contempt. Just ahead of us, outside the town, down the train tracks, we see what looks like a factory with tall smokestacks, still with dirty smoke drifting up. We figured it must be a munitions factory the way it was isolated, set up with walls all around it. But as we got closer, it was like the place gave out these vibrations that beat on your ear drums. My heart started racing. I pin all my troubles on that place. Every step I took was like there was no ground under my feet and my boots could go down deep into air. And the smell was real stink. I will never forget it. Sometimes I think I still smell it on my skin when I wake up in the morning, and I shower and scrub myself with Irish Spring and a brush till I'm red. That's how bad it is."

Is it something like the smell that lies under the disinfectant in all the hospital rooms? Melba thought she might actually have asked this question; the story drew her in with such tentacles. She didn't want to hear what she suspected was coming next, but she was trapped as surely as those who waited inside the prison walls.

Kenji absently continued his massage. "And something else. Something so evil it smelled its own unmistakable smell -- sulfuric -- but that's too clean for it. Once you smell it, you know it. You recognize it, like a place you've never been before but you know it because you need to know it for your survival.

"Nobody talked as we crept up to the sooty red brick walls. Everything was squat and thick. There was no sun. I remember that. The sun did not shine. There was nobody in the guard towers. It was so quiet it was like something was about to explode. The Germans were either waiting in ambush inside those walls, or they were gone. All along the front they were retreating. But we don't take any chances. We got our bayonets drawn. The entrance is a corridor between two brick walls, a perfect trap. We're watching every angle at once, and as we get to the gate, I swear I heard howls. Wolf howls, Dracula howls, wings flapping, clouds gathering as we rushed the gate. It wasn't even locked. We go in, and Melba, oh Melba, what we seen. All these skeletons looking at us, moving skeletons, bald and dressed in black and white striped rags. Cannot tell man or woman. They move toward us, slowly. They smell. They have tears in their sunken eyes. They are reaching out their bony hands, their stick arms at us. All the guys break out their rations while the captain tells us take it easy. Take it slow. Give them just a little or they die, their stomachs no more used to eating. Some guys, they sit down and take one skeleton in their arms, like it was a baby and feed it with a spoon. But most of us, we don't do that. We're afraid of them. That's the truth. And they're afraid of us, like we're some new joke, some greater cruelty the Germans have dreamed up. We put our food down on the ground for them and we back away. Speaking for myself, I was afraid they were contagious. Not that they have a disease, but that they are sickness itself, they are

115

death and I don't want one of them to touch me. I caught myself holding my own arms. I was afraid that once they started to eat, they wouldn't stop and it would be too horrible for words, an orgy, a cannibalistic orgy. I'm so ashamed of myself, Melba. You always think that if you see someone really hungry, you will give that person everything in your pocket. I did that, broke out every scrap of rations and gave a woman my cash. But I didn't want anyone to touch me. So we go into the barracks, and there's more of them there. The place reeked of rot and sewage, urine and sickness and death. You breathe it into your lungs and it stays there for the rest of your life, and with every breath you take you know what the human race is capable of. I had to go outside so I didn't puke.

"I take Mitts Sasabuchi and we head for what we figure is the office space for this hell. We'll round up the paperwork. We find a desk piled with shoes, all kine shoes – good leather boots, wooden shoes – you know - the Dutch kine, children's shoes, some with braces on them. Some are already sorted by size. There are bins full of human hair, one bin grey and kinda stiff looking, another fine and soft, gold and dark like little kid hair. I see boxes of eyeglasses, stacks of winter coats bundled and addressed to Berlin. Mitts and me don't look at each other. We need air. We go outside and start walking across this field. It's so cold, we're shivering. At the far end is this concrete building that looks like a prison bathhouse, but it's not water that comes out of the showerheads. It's gas, of course. This is where the Nazis gas these people. Then they take them to this other building. The oven was still warm. I touched it. Put my hand on the warm concrete, but I cannot look inside. I walk outside. There are bodies stacked in back like cordwood, bleached and stiff. I cannot believe I am awake. I turn away. And then I cannot walk. I sit down and I cry like one girl.

"How can people do things like that? I will never, never understand it. It's one thing to kill someone in battle, not that I'm excusing it, but I did it. I understand it. But to kill people like it's your career. You get up in the morning and go to work and this is your work and you have a lunch break and after lunch you gas and burn more men, women and children, fill out the quota forms, tag the coats, bag the hair and you call it a day and go home and have your supper and a beer and maybe read the sports page and you shower and get into your pajamas and into your bed. Do you say your prayers? Do you dare turn out the light? Do you make love? Yes, that you do, that you do. You caress your wife softly, as if she is the only tenderness in the world. You touch her with your filthy, killing hands. Then maybe you sleep.

Do you dream?" Kenji's hands stopped moving.

Melba wanted to cry out, *"Whatever you do, don't say my name. Let me escape."* Silent and unmoving, she yearned for one thing -- annihilation. But she was trapped close to the surface of light, as if pinioned under glass, begging. *Don't give me your dreams. Or I'll give you mine.*

CHAPTER ELEVEN

In which a terrible legacy is bequeathed

Melba was always the first one home from school. In the good old days, before her eleventh birthday when bombs fell on Hawai'i, she would have the house all to herself, for twenty minutes, sometimes thirty. In the quiet, she would notice the coolness of the linoleum floor against her bare feet, the snug yet airy closeness of the dear walls, the little suction pop of the ice box door as she opened it to reach for the striped glass pitcher of Kool-Aid. With her drink beside her, she would curl up in her father's big old chair, able to smell his myriad and comforting aromas: tobacco, shaving cream, the sea. She would open her library book and read in utter peace until she heard the twins clattering up the steps. They'd tumble in, sunny and careless, having stopped for every gecko spied on a hedge, every new item in a store window, practically every stray plumeria blossom fallen in their path. Their hair was always damp and their fingers sticky. They would need immediate Kool-Aid. The last to come home would be Peter and Raymond. They had sports and packs of friends, and Roosevelt High School was two buses away. Oka-san, of course, would still be at Matsufuji-san's and Oto-san would already be on his boat, preparing for a night on the ocean.

Life in Hawai'i was now divided into two parts – before Pearl Harbor and after. Now when Melba came home from school, she would find her father sitting in his chair, haloed by the immaculate white doilies her mother daily placed on the chair back and arms before leaving for the tofu factory. He would be shirtless, the room stuffy, the curtains drawn. The sharp smell of sake or the yeasty fragrance of beer, one or the other, sometimes both would hover in the air. He often smoked and she would have to be careful not to cough. Meekly, so as to attract little attention, head bowed, Melba would tip-toe in, being careful not to let the screen door thwack, and greet her father in her most inoffensive, most deferential voice, *"Tadaima, Oto-san."*

He didn't acknowledge her anymore, not a nod, not a grunt, not a glance. Gratefully, she would go straight to the kitchen and begin supper preparations, taking a long time to slice the vegetables and an age to wash the rice so she could stay in the kitchen until the others came home. She listened for the twins singing, would hear them stop just outside the door, recognize that uniquely feminine form of servility that was almost another language as they greeted their father in unison, then darted away before he might contaminate their spirits. Glowing with life and perspiration, they would tumble into the kitchen where Melba had two glasses of Kool-Aid poured.

When the brothers came home, Raymond, his eyes on the floor, would grunt his *"Tadaima,"* then go straight to his room. Melba could never tell if he was angry or scared. Peter always sat down and talked to Oto-san in Japanese. It was like talking to an invalid. It was an act of mercy only the eldest son dared perform. And Oto-san always looked at Peter as if he was going to cry. Seeing her father like this frightened Melba more than the Japanese bombs.

As Melba and Sweetie turned the corner into Ka`a`ai Street, Melba felt her insides coil into knots that had become painfully familiar on approaching home. It was a fight to keep her food in her stomach where it belonged. She dreaded climbing the front steps, opening the door and seeing her father, glowering dimly in his chair, more and more like Uncle Hideshi, his silence laced with menace. At the hibiscus hedge she paused. She wanted Sweetie to linger, to talk, to delay the moment she must enter the house, but Sweetie said her Mama Nui, her father's mother, was visiting from Hana and she wanted to get home. "Mama Nui make da best *kulolo*, not too rubbery like da kine. She teaching me to

quilt. Hoooo, take one long time for do one small part."
And Sweetie left, skipping, home to immense brown
grandmother arms and slices of sweet *kulolo*.

Melba entered her yard. Something was wrong.
She looked at the house. It throbbed. It seemed to grow
and tilt toward her. The hair on her arms stood up. A
shiver passed along her spine. She glanced at her
brooding mango tree as if for strength or escape. It
seemed to be holding its ancient arboreal breath. She
walked dutifully, slowly toward the front door, aware of
a trembling behind her ears, her heart pounding. Up the
steps. She creaked open the door. Her father was not in
his chair. Something smelled, like someone forgot to
flush the toilet. Gingerly she stepped into the dim light,
as if the floor was made of glass. "Oto-san?" She
listened. The silence beat in her ears. *"Tadaima, Oto-
san."* The door to her parents' bedroom was closed. It
was never closed. "Oto-san?" Her hand fluttered as she
touched the bedroom doorknob. The door opened easily,
lightly, when she had expected some enormous pressure.
It swung back. Her father hung from the ceiling fan. She
gasped, turned away, her books falling. She ran out of
the house. "Sweetie, Sweetie." But Sweetie was gone.
She hurried to one side of the yard and then the other. "I
must calm down. I must think." She wanted to run for
her mother. She started for the street and remembered

that if she left, Avis and Hazel would come home and see what she had seen. She walked in little circles around her mango tree, first in one direction and then the other. She heard the twins before she saw them. They were singing, "Oh Susannah." They had been singing it since they learned it, driving everyone crazy. She hurried to the hibiscus hedge, placed herself outside it. They were holding hands, swinging arms, "... now don't you cry for me, for I come from Alabama with my banjo on my knee ...." They stopped when they saw Melba.

Melba told them, "Oto-san very sick. Very sick. Go to Matsufuji Tofu and tell Oka-san come home now. Oto-san very very sick. Hurry." She took their books. They raced away. She put their books on the porch steps and sat beside them, exhausted. She could not go back inside the house. She would sit there forever if need be.

She saw Peter's head over the hibiscus. He was with his friends. Raymond was about six paces behind but entered the yard first because Peter continued to talk with his friends. Melba looked up at Raymond and began to cry and couldn't stop, her sobs convulsing her small body, the house, the world. "Oto-san, Oto-san." She looked toward the house in agony.

Peter broke from his friends. He ran up the steps past them as if he already knew. She tried to grab his leg, to spare him. She cried, *"Oto-san ma`ke."*

He almost tripped, but didn't stop. Raymond sat down beside her. She stopped crying but was still shaking. They listened.

Peter came back out slowly. He leaned against the porch pillar. His face was slack and sallow. "Go get Mama," he said to Melba.

"I awreddy sent Hazel, Avis. They dunno. I tell them Oto-san very sick."

"Raymond, you go get Uncle Hideshi."

Raymond gave Melba a hug. He went in the house, was there for only an instant, then walked away with long quick strides, head bowed.

Peter called after him, "Hurry. We got the curfew."

Raymond began to run, his head up, his fists pumping. He looked splendid, like an athlete.

Melba was astonished at his speed. Not until he rounded the corner, did she speak. In a whisper, she asked Peter. "Should we call the police?"

"We'll wait for Uncle Hideshi. He'll know what to do. This isn't a good time for anyone Japanese to need the police."

The alarming implications of their situation crowded in on them. Peter began to pace the porch. "Here comes Mama."

Melba stood up. It was difficult to recognize her

mother from afar – her walk was completely different now that she wore American dresses and shoes. She was practically running. The twins were half a block behind, no longer singing.

Peter walked down the steps slowly to greet her.

She looked at him, raised her hand to her mouth. Peter put his arm around her. She wrenched away from him. He tried to block the door.

With a fierceness that startled Peter, but which Melba recognized with gladness as woman power, their mother pushed Peter out of the way, not with a shove, but a fierce look. She went instinctively toward the bedroom and let out one long loud wail. She rushed to the kitchen, yanked open a drawer and grabbed the large fish-cleaning knife. Moving in a crazed frenzy that defied intervention, she stalked back to the bedroom, kicked Melba's fallen books out of the way, righted the chair, climbed on it, and started sawing at the rope, a thick hairy old rope from the sampan. She gasped air, grunted, cried out, her black eyes wild. She was unearthly, something terrible. Swirling winds surrounded her, energy charged from her.

Melba stayed in the doorway, unable to move, blocking the twins. They were crying. Raymond arrived, out of breath, shiny with sweat. She stepped aside.

"I went to Duc Kee Store," he said, "and they let

me use the telephone. Uncle Hideshi coming." He looked at their mother in awe as she hacked away in a fury of frustration.

At the sight of Raymond, Peter, who had been rendered immobile, said gently, firmly, "Mama, let us. We are his sons. It is our responsibility."

She froze, then allowed herself to be helped from the chair. Peter relieved her of the knife, got on the chair, nodded to Raymond who put his arms about his father's torso, then with one deft stroke sliced the rope clean. Their father's body fell over Raymond's shoulders. He staggered under the weight, might have fallen, but Oka-san leaned into him, supporting him.

They laid Oto-san on the bed and Oka-san bent over him, furious and cold. Peter took her by both arms and for a moment, just the briefest moment, she folded into her son's comfort.

Melba led the twins to the kitchen. They were quiet and reverential as she poured them their Kool-Aid. Raymond rushed past them to the bathroom. They heard him being sick to his stomach. He was in there forever.

Oka-san beckoned to Melba and the twins. Her arms enfolding Avis and Hazel, weren't long enough for Melba, too. Melba understood, but had never felt so alone in her life. She turned and walked out the door. Raymond emerged shirtless, saw her and called her name.

    "S'okay," she said, "I going to my mango tree."

    She climbed up. She was not crying. She felt the familiar roughness of the bark, knew every knob and branch, climbed up to the breeze, where the tree limbs rocked like a cradle.

    We not enough for him. He no more love us enough to stay no matter what. Didn't he know we would go to jail wid him? Pack our bags go mauka and hide wid him? We even go to Tokyo wid him. Why he do dis? Why li-dis? He could jump offa da Pali. Go hang in a forest. Why here? He know I wen be da first what come home from school. He know I be the one what find him. Why a father do dis to his little daughter? He must really hate me. I must be one awful girl.

CHAPTER TWELVE

In which the Buddha who packs heat pays a visit.

Who is this large dark person, this enormous comfort in whose shade I lie as if beneath my mango tree?

Melba drifted toward the rounded sorrowing form beside the bed, the bowed head, the lips that moved slightly, the clasped hands. The man was not aware of her nearness and yet he guarded her stick of a body, lying helplessly pinioned between clean sheets. With his murmurings he guarded her soul, strewing prayers like petals in her path, raising up unseen armies to make safe her steps in perilous territory. She curled her spirit back into her rigid body, like a cat in a basket and slept in utter peace.

How long?

Unwillingly, she moved from sleep and boundless serenity toward walls and tubes and needles that hurt. She almost surfaced, broke through the scrim, then retreated in panic. The light caused pain. It was like being shoved against a giant ginger grater that scraped her skin raw -- that's how much the light hurt. She needed to see if the guardian was still there, the one praying. She didn't need to see details, just the dark ponderous shadow sitting rounded beside her bed. A Buddha shape. She gazed fondly at him as if through softly rippling water. He wore a dark blue uniform, a shield of gold over his heart, I know him well. He has a gun. I can trust him. My son.

Melba sank once more into silence and safety. She drifted away, arms out as if flying, a leaf carried by breezes through air, tumbling happily into water, dancing down, beautifully down where there was no light, no sound, no burden. No safety. No being.

Which way to the Buddha?

CHAPTER THIRTEEN

In which Melba arrives at a new home in a
banana patch and watches a cousin march off to
fight the divine emperor.

Blackout was no problem deep in Manoa Valley,
way in the back of Uncle Hideshi's banana farm, where
the Yamadas had moved. The monkeypod, the *iliahi*, the
guava, mountain apple, eucalyptus and *hau* trees were so
thick and tangled, their canopy so dense, Melba thought
that if she were to set fire to their little one-room shack
in the middle of the night, no enemy airplane would even
see a spark.

Melba told this to Sweetie at school. "But the fire
no burn," she added with a huge sigh of weariness, "Alla
time rain, rain, rain."

"Got wailele?"

"Um hum. One big one – Manoa Falls."

"Can swim?"

"I dunno know. We nevah once go deah. Too
busy das why."

Everything about Sweetie was vibrant,
unquenchable. She was one of those children who stand

out in a class of fifty, whose spirit shines right through their eyes, innocent and daring, provoking adults to wonder sadly what will become of her. She asked, "I can come?"

Melba considered it a moment then said, "As one long walk, you know. All trew mud."

Sweetie became even more excited, "Ask your mama-san I can come. Stay da night."

"Okay."

But Melba didn't ask. Her mother had become so busy and unapproachable that Melba felt as though she had lost two parents, not one. Matsufuji-san was back in business and Mama worked dawn till night. She didn't need to remind the children that she was lucky to have work with so many Japanese let go from their jobs. They knew this, and they knew she was all they had.

If Mama was not home by dark, one of the children would take a lantern and meet her on the trail. Usually Peter.

As soon as she walked in the door, the twins scrambled to arrange her black shoes on the steps, toes outward, the way she liked them. The first thing she did, every evening upon coming home was test the rice that Melba had cooked. She was never satisfied although she didn't say so. Melba could tell by the little crinkle between her brows, the straight lips, the abruptness with

which she replaced the pot lid, then checked the fire.
With a critical glance she inspected the vegetables the
twins picked from the new vegetable garden and which
Melba had carefully sliced, every slice the same, thin
and diagonal and arranged in neat piles. Melba had
grated the ginger and mounded it on a little blue and
white dish. She used to pile it precisely in the middle,
but noticed that Mama would always move it a little to
one side before scraping it into the wok, so now Melba
mounded it just off center. Without the smallest nod of
approval, Mama turned to root in the wood box for more
kindling for the fire. She carried the wood, the twins
carried the vegetables and ginger and Melba had the
honor of the wok, which she had prepared with sesame
oil.

Mama set the wok on the outdoor grill which
Raymond had fired, and she whipped up her nightly
magic. The children listened to the sizzle, smelled the
burst of onion and ginger, watched the rising steam, and
relaxed into grand and fragrant vapors. Their mother was
home and in charge, and they were reassured.

They ate indoors, sitting on tatami mats around a
low table, which they pushed against the wall when they
were finished. That was when they felt the presence of
Oto-san, when they sat together and ate warm food. He
was there among them, presiding over the meal, unseen,

but breathing his despair on them, his breath hot and malevolent. Because they dared not speak of this or of him, they ate in silence, *hashi* clicking against bowls. They heard each other chewing, breathing. They could almost hear their eyelids blinking.

Even the twins ate quietly with heads bowed, side by side, shiny black hair hanging in curtains around their identical faces. It was not until Avis and Hazel were back outdoors doing the dishes in the big washtub that they resumed their chatter, singing like little birds, privately happy, "Ai, ai, ai, ai, come to your window, ere moonlight fails and the starlight pales ...," they sang softly, barely disturbing the gloom. You had to listen for them, especially if wind was stealing through the trees, clicking the bamboo and palms, or if the armies of giant toads were drumming their mating calls, sounding like the night marchers, the ghosts of fallen warriors moving along their eternally appointed paths, dispensing woe, drowning out small voices singing "Cielito Lindo" in the dark jungle.

How could Melba bring Sweetie home to this?

When Sweetie inquired, "What your mama-san say?"

Melba lied. "She tinking."

*

Every afternoon Melba retrieved Hazel and Avis

from their classes, then they'd ride the bus together to the end of the line at Manoa Road. From there, they walked until the road ended in a wide dirt lane. This was where Uncle Hideshi parked his big green truck, off to the side beneath a banyan tree bigger than a garage. The path went over a footbridge across Aihualama Stream into a patch of sunlight and tall ginger, then into the dim forest. The jungle trail had been carved out by the Hawaiians in the old days and laid with large smooth round stones. The girls removed their *geta*, because the wooden sandals got caught in the chinks of the rocks. Also, the *geta* would sink in the mud and get lost when they veered off the ancient way onto the dirt trail leading to Uncle Hideshi's farm. If it was raining, the girls picked giant ape leaves for umbrellas. It was hard to balance all this and their gas masks as they crossed streams and climbed over tree roots and rocks. When they passed Uncle's nice white house, Auntie Junko always waved to them, as if she looked out the window all day long waiting for them to come along. Sometimes she called them for *senbei* and milk or gave them a jar of *tsukemono* she had just made to take home. The twins were always delighted. Melba was quietly resentful. Did Auntie Junko think Mama couldn't make *senbei* or *tsukemono* just because her heavy *tsukemono* stone sat idly in its wooden bucket? She was mostly resentful that she had to live way in back of the bananas in the mean little shack with no closets so everything had to hang on the walls, in baskets and buckets, while her cousins lived in a house with bedrooms and a kitchen and closets, the way she used to live.

Oto-san really hate us.

*

Melba reminded Hazel and Avis, as they sat with Auntie Junko, before they could ask for seconds, that they had chores to do at home. They gulped milk, bowed with mouths full, and ran ahead, gas masks bouncing against their hips.

Melba never forgot her first sight of the dark rickety shack on its stilts, the steps broken, the screens torn, everything made worse by the horrible knowledge that she would be living there. Inside, furry mold dotted the ceiling. It looked like the sky over Pearl Harbor the day the war began. Worst of all, big hairy centipedes with not a hundred, but seemingly a thousand slinky feet crept about. They reared up on a dozen or so hind legs and lunged at the broom as Peter or Raymond jabbed, then moved in for the kill, the twins shrieking, clutching each other, faces into each other's breast, eyes sneaking peeks. Once, Hazel woke up screaming in the middle of the night with a centipede on the back of her hand. The creature was horrible but almost holy with moonlight on

its back. Peter quickly scooped up Hazel, rushed her
outdoors, and in one swift gesture, swept the centipede
into the night. Amazingly, Hazel had not been bitten. But
she had centipede dreams for years, her screams ripping
open the night.

Mice also came to call, but Mama and the boys
found their holes and patched them, and they mended the
screens and stairs. Cousin Hideo brought a couple of
cans of pale green paint, left-over, he said, from painting
latrines for the army, and he helped paint the outside of
the shack. There wasn't enough for inside, so the walls
were still dark unfinished wood.

Cousin Hideo had tried to enlist in the army and
go to war, but because he was Japanese, he was turned
away, so he joined the Varsity Victory Volunteers,
which meant he did a lot of hard dirty work for the army
for free.

Hideo was not very tall, but he had a wide chest
and impressive arms and shoulders from carrying
bananas. Muscles seemed to finger right up from his
scalp into his thick black hair so that the hairs popped
straight to attention. An especially rebellious clump
above his right brow awarded him a rakish and
endearing air. Except for his hair, he might have been in
danger of being too handsome. His cheerfulness made
even his grouchy father smile, or perhaps Uncle Hideshi

smiled because Hideo managed to squeeze more action into a minute than most people even thought about. He was so good natured, his younger, slower brothers, Ryozo and Isami, couldn't resent him. They teased him unmercifully, but affectionately when they found out that his Varsity Victory friends called him, "Skippy."

Hideo just grinned and told his brothers, "Call me anything but don't call me late for dinner." All the while he wielded his machete and piled up the bananas, never stopping. He whistled and sang as he worked. Therefore, Hazel and Avis loved him. It seemed to be mutual. He always had a treat for them, gum or sour balls, and sometimes candy cigarettes.

They tried to whistle like Hideo as they did their chores, descending on the vegetable garden after school, armed with buckets and digging sticks for the weeds. Their whistling, however, was not loud enough to suit them, so they went back to singing.

"Be careful the seedlings," Melba called. When they were finished weeding the vegetables, the twins swept the tatami in the house, then scrubbed the steps, all the time singing, whistling and humming, completely unaware of the happiness they bestowed with their double sunny faces, twenty busy pudgy fingers. Everyone indulged them and allowed them to be careless.

Every day Melba lit a fire under the tall wooden hot water tank which Uncle Hideshi and his sons helped Peter and Raymond build. They lined it with an old metal cylinder Uncle found at the Kailua dump on one of his trips. They also built an enclosed shower stall nearby.

When the water got warm, Melba poured some in buckets, took it to the wash tub on the side of the house and did the laundry. She put hot coals in the iron, and ironed what she had washed the day before, so everyone would have clean clothes in the morning. Raymond provided the wood for the fire. He was also in charge of the outhouse and the animals.

Mama invested in six chickens, a rooster, and four rabbits, which nicely multiplied. Raymond and Peter built cages for them. Raymond cleaned the cages, gathered the eggs, and fed the animals. And it was Raymond who had to kill them at the appropriate times. He got good at it. One strong twist of a chicken's neck and it was practically ready for the pot. To dispatch a rabbit, he held it by the ears with one hand and with the other hand wacked it with a bat on the back of its head, face away. He only did this when the twins were not around.

Peter went off into the forest every day with a huge sack, and when it was so full of ti leaves and fern that he could barely carry it, he came home. He washed the greens, then tied his wild harvest into neat bundles with banana fiber and splashed them with water. He rose before dawn and quietly left the house with his sack of greenery and his school books. He walked all the way to school, peddling bits of the forest at flower shops, lei stands and markets along the way. He had a regular route. He was a good salesman.

On Saturdays, the whole family worked for Uncle Hideshi. Melba and the twins picked the tiny flowers off the tips of each green banana on each stalk so the bananas would grow sweeter and fuller. By the end of the day, Melba's arms ached from reaching up and her thumb hurt from pinching. Hazel and Avis tried to help, but they were short and easily distracted. They were also incapacitated by the sight of big sugarcane spiders and positively paralyzed by the dreaded centipedes. Uncle and the boys cut the stalks of ripening bananas and carried them on their shoulders all the way to the truck. Mama and Auntie Junko picked the vegetables, sorted and bundled them, and these, too, were carried by the boys to the truck at the head of the trail. Hideo always worked the hardest and everyone had to pick up the slack once he joined the Varsity Victory Volunteers.

Even at school, the war imposed its labors on the children. The upper grades were taken by truck once a week to work in the pineapple fields. All children had to dig and maintain trenches for shelter in case the Japanese returned on another bombing raid. If the enemy came on a rainy day, the casualties would be great, for the trenches regularly filled with water. It was known that submarines prowled Hawaiian seas and continued to sink ships. Hilo, Kahului and Nawiliwili harbors were sometimes shelled. Japanese planes returned in March, in the dead of night. Luckily dense clouds protected Oahu and most of their bombs landed offshore. One load however, fell on Tantalus, just above Roosevelt High School. It awakened the family. "It's thunder," Peter said. They listened for rain and heard it coming on the leaves and were satisfied.

The next day, when they learned how close bombs had come to Manoa, that the Japanese planes had probably flown right over their house while they slept, Uncle Hideshi predicted "*Nippon ga katsu.*" Japan will win. He said it with his arms folded across his chest, his short legs wide apart, then swaggered away to work with unusual vigor, wielding his machete on encroaching *haole koa* saplings.

After the Tantalus raid, the children entertained brief hopes that the schools would again close. They didn't, and Melba could not escape Sweetie. Finally, reluctantly, the visit was arranged. She would come on Friday and stay the weekend.

Sweetie, wearing a starched red and white mu'umu'u and big white hair ribbons, came laden with gifts. She didn't realize how long and dirty the walk would be, even though Melba had warned her in excruciating detail. Sweetie had two cans of tuna fish, a roll of toilet paper, a beautiful *honohono* orchid trailing clouds of lavender on its long hanging stems, and a box of Mama Nui's *kulolo*. Plus, her books and gas mask. She managed on the bus and was okay on the road. By the time they got to the trail, however, the orchid seemed to have put on weight.

Hazel said, "If we hang a *honohono* in a tree, it will be very very happy to go wild."

Avis offered, "And I carry da *kulolo*. If we eat some, no be so heavy."

"I help you."

Melba was embarrassed by their laziness, by the hardship of the walk, by the depth of the mud. But they lightened the load a little by eating the top layer of *kulolo*, tasting wonderfully of coconut, sugar, and taro. Sweetie insisted on carrying the *honohono* the whole way herself. She allowed Melba to relieve her of her gas mask.

They had just passed through the *hau* thicket into a patch of sunlight when Sweetie stopped, "Look. Ovah deah." She put down her bundles on some tree roots, being careful to spread out the long stems of the *honohono* like a skirt. "Look, you got shampoo ginger." She reached for the round crimson heads.

Melba asked, "Wha'dat?"

"In a shower, you squeeze em on a head. See?" She clenched one red globe in her fist, and thick sweet smelling white liquid burst out and ran down her arm. She wiped it on her mud-spattered mu'umu'u, then proceeded to pick more. When the twins deposited their bundles to help gather, Sweetie cautioned, "Don't pick more dan you can use. Everyting what we pick, we hafta use."

Melba was fascinated in spite of herself. "How we carry em?"

Hazel said, "In a *kulolo* box."

They all laughed, sat down on the tree roots and ate the rest of the *kulolo*. They then stuffed the box with red globes of ginger. Melba said, "We can give some to Auntie Junko onna way home."

Auntie was waiting for them. Knowing they would be bringing a visitor, she prepared *kinako mochi* with *azuki* beans, and *mochi* stuffed with sweet lima beans. Melba was proud to have a gift of shampoo ginger for her.

*

Sweetie loved the small green shack in the back

of the bananas. "It like one secret house in a forest." She loved the animals, especially the new baby rabbits.

Melba said "We eat 'em."

"Still can love 'em."

While the others did their chores, Sweetie busied herself gathering *laua'e* fern and yellow ginger. She strung the ginger into a lei which she placed around the lantern on the table, and she laid the fern flat, one leaf overlapping another in a line running the length of the table. The house smelled like happiness.

When Mama came home, she actually smiled. In honor of having a guest she had bought candied lotus root, and, most miraculous of all, chocolate-drizzled long johns.

At the supper table, Sweetie asked a thousand questions about the waterfall, the forest, gathering guava. She told them about Anuenue, the goddess of the rainbow, who lives in Manoa Valley. The children stuffed themselves on sweets, sucked the cream from the long johns, licked the chocolate, pictured the beautiful lady with rainbows all around her.

With great importance, as if he had participated in the decision, Peter announced that the government had changed its mind and Japanese Americans were now allowed to join the fight. They all cheered. Peter added, "Hideo already signed up." They clapped.

Melba saw Raymond look furtively at Peter and then their mother. He was the only one not happy. But he smiled when he saw Melba watching him. She knew it was only because he didn't want to spoil the party. He just couldn't help it. A glance at the perpetual slump of his shoulders, the way his neck stuck out as if his head was too heavy, was a reminder of why they were here, making the best of it in a latrine green shack courtesy of grouchy slave-driver Uncle Hideshi.

*

This Saturday, the girls were excused from their banana duties to entertain their guest. They took Sweetie to Manoa Falls. She, without a moment's hesitation, stripped off her clothes and waded into the plunge pool, shrieking, slipping on soft golden moss, laughing. The Yamada girls looked at each other, embarrassed.

"Come on in." Sweetie screamed. Her invitation echoed on the valley walls. The twins simultaneously turned their faces to Melba, raised their eyebrows and bit their lips, begging. She had to smile. In seconds, all three Yamada girls were bare and howling with a most exhilarating abandon. They struggled against the force of the water and the slipperiness of the bottom, pulling each other forward, following Sweetie to the falls. The water, cascading in clear torrents, pounded their heads and shoulders. Melba had never felt so fine and free in her whole life. They washed their hair with shampoo ginger, then dressed and stretched out on big warm rocks in the sun. When their hair dried, it was so soft and sweet smelling, they kept bringing locks of it under their noses and inhaling deeply, with tremendous pleasure.

While they were warm and happy, Sweetie, lying on her back looking into the canopy, spotted a young mango tree in the tangle of jungle across the stream. It was tall and spindly, trying to reach the sun through the larger more exuberant trees surrounding it. Its leaves were dusty and darkest green. It had no fruit. But it was a mango tree for her best friend. She waded across the stream, the Yamada girls watching her. She turned around, triumphantly pointing, "Look, Melba. For you. One mango tree."

The twins rushed across the water. Melba approached thoughtfully. "Poor ting. Not much of a mango tree." She walked around it, appraising it. Aware of Sweetie's anxious eyes, she reached out and touched the tree's smooth bark, ran her hand up and down. Then, mostly for Sweetie, she put her arms around it, leaned into its needy trunk and embraced it. At first, she felt nothing, as expected, then little by little, warmth seeped into her limbs, her chest, her heart, and peace insinuated itself from the top of her head down to her muddy toes. She smiled.

The twins rolled their eyes and began to sing, to the tune of *O Tannenbaum*, "Oh mango tree, oh mango tree, how lovely God has made thee ..." They faltered, scrambling for more words, laughing. Melba and Sweetie joined in, Melba still leaning a shoulder against the tree. Sweetie moved her hands and arms in hula gestures, swaying like the thin tree in a breeze. They picked *palapalae* ferns and Sweetie wove them into a lei and draped it over the lowest mango branch, thanking God for the life of the tree.

On the way home, Sweetie scouted the places in the stream where fish were likely to sleep, and on Sunday morning the girls rose early, tip-toed to the shady inlets and Sweetie, moving swiftly, picked the drowsy fish right out of their watery beds. She managed to get two before the others darted away in panic, alerting the entire Aihualama Stream clear down to the University of Hawai'i campus.

Mama cooked the fish with *shoyu* and lots of green onion and ginger slivers. Yesterday's ginger lei, wilted, but still encircling the lantern, was more fragrant than the evening before. Mama smiled again. That was twice since Oto-san died.

Everyone was sorry when Sweetie left. Sadness again fell about their shoulders as the legacy of Oto-san's choice resumed its tyranny, making them mute to each other and blind and deaf, too.

The small green hope implanted in Melba's heart by Sweetie's visit began its slow transformation into anger, empowering and possessive. It felt good.

Whenever she could, which was not very often, she made her way to the falls, crossed the stream and sat beside her stunted mango tree, struggling toward the sun.

I hate him. I will not let him wreck my life. I am good.

*

The day of cousin Hideo's induction into the army, the whole family piled in the truck and drove downtown. The sidewalks on King Street were packed with people, excited and helpless before the whirlwind that engulfed the world and that now dipped down and personally selected each one of them for suffering in the way a tornado fingers one farmhouse and spares another.

The sun shone and blowsy white clouds feathered the sky. A dark-haired *haole* lady passed out little American flags. Melba clutched hers fiercely to her chest. She couldn't sort out her emotions. One of them was shame and that puzzled her. Uncle Hideshi alone turned away as if he didn't see the *haole* lady, her pretty smile, her outstretched arm, the tiny flag fluttering toward him. Not even for his son, on this day of days, when it was again fine to be Japanese, would he betray

Japan with the smallest gesture. Uncle Hideshi would never compromise. He would be shot rather than stomp on Emperor Hirohito's face, and there was something to be admired in that. Melba looked at the man, brother to her father, and wished she liked him.

Was that music?

Everyone turned, straining toward the oncoming band, the drums and bugles, the xylophone. They leaned into the street for the first glimpse of the parade of Hawai`i boys going away to war. The parade flowed down King Street in a sea of khaki, streams of young men in crisp new uniforms. They turned smartly left into the iron gates of Iolani Palace with the royal crests that read, *"Ua mau ke ea o ka aina I ka pono"* – the life of the land is perpetuated in righteousness.

Melba's mother reached out and put her arm around Auntie Junko's waist as Hideo passed, face straight ahead, but looking side-eye at them, a smile in his eyes. Melba looked around. Did anyone else feel what she was feeling? Were they all bewitched by the marching band and gay bunting? Did they hear the ground tremble? Did they look at all those gleaming faces and wonder which ones have no future? Why was this acceptable? Her ears rang with the pounding of her blood. And this, she realized, was her answer: We are lifted from the ordinary and transported to a larger stage, with music, costumes, the rush of foreboding and happiness that comes before the curtain rises on the drama with its shabby set that looks magical from the cheap seats.

The palace grounds filled up with thousands of *nisei* soldiers, each wearing a paper lei made by Hawaii's schoolchildren, as they promised to fulfill their duties to God and country. Will the Buddha go into battle with them, sitting lotus in a far-away place? Impassive? She could no longer find Hideo, also known as Skippy, in the rows and rows of soldiers lined up in front of the palace. He was lost to them. The new soldiers marched away, flags flying, music swelling into a crescendo.

*

A week later, Peter heard from Varsity Victory Brigade sources that Hideo and the rest of his company would be going by train from Schofield Barracks to the Iwilei station, then marched to Pier 11 to board the *Lurline* and sail to the mainland for basic training, then the war. This was one last chance to see him before he left. The twins and Melba strung double plumeria leis. Aunty Junko packed a tin *bento* box full of Hideo's favorites, Spam *musubi*, *takuan*, chicken *katsu* and her homemade *tsukemono*. The family was again loaded into the truck. Hideo would be so surprised they had found out about this secret troop movement.

Apparently, most of Honolulu heard the same military secret, for the *makai* side of the road was so jammed with people carrying leis and *bento* boxes that *haole* soldiers had to be deployed for crowd control, to keep everyone on the sidewalk.

The sun withered the crowds. The Hawai'i men, when they came marching down the *makai* side of the boulevard, carried huge duffle bags. Some men were limping. Army shoes were too narrow for EEE luau feet. Cries went up from the crowd. Aloha, goodbye, *sayonara*. A mother tried to break free to hug her son as he passed. She was shoved back. Leis were thrown to the men, flowers sailing in the air like a carnival ring-toss. Isami spotted Hideo first, "He coming." The family surged forward. The *haole* soldiers pushed them back, shouting at them. Auntie Junko helplessly kissed Hideo with her eyes.

Suddenly Avis grabbed the *bento* box from her aunt's hands and the twins scooted under the soldiers' rifles, ran right up to Hideo and handed him his lunch. They held up their leis, unable to reach his neck. He bent to receive them and as he did, a *haole* soldier bellowed, "Move along, move along, eyes front." Hideo straightened up, wearing flowers, and marched away. Everyone cheered as Avis and Hazel, suddenly shy, darted back to the family.

*

On the day they got the word that cousin Hideo was killed, Melba went to sit alone under her spindly mango tree by the waterfall. She leaned wearily against it, unable to climb into its thin arms for fear of breaking them. Cousin Hideo was one of the first, but did not have the distinction of being the very first, *nisei* to die in the war. He was killed in Salerno, Italy on Hill 600 when someone tripped something called a Bouncing Betty.

Melba wished she could share her tree with Auntie Junko because she was afraid that grief would silence her aunt, steal her laughter, etch a grim unforgiving line where her smile should be, as it had done to Mama.

Instead, Auntie Junko talked and talked, to whoever was in the room, to the walls, to the trees outside her window. She rocked as she talked, back and forth, hands folded in her lap, her eyes filling with tears that never fell. She spoke in Japanese every detail of her eldest son's brief life. Uncle Hideshi could not listen. He stomped out into the yard. He glared at his other sons resentfully and they hunched away from him.

That night, Raymond said to Melba, "If the war lasts until I'm old enough to go, I won't. I won't fight in their army. Not when they're locking up Japanese-

Americans on the Mainland. Not after what they did to our family."

Until that moment, Melba thought he had been bewitched by the parade, the band and flags. She was glad she hadn't been alone in her puzzling feelings the day Hideo marched away. She waited for her brother to elaborate.

"When they took our father's sampan," he said, "they took his life."

She turned away and couldn't look at him she was so disappointed. When she spoke, it was in a whisper, barely audible, "I wish they shoot Oto-san in his sampan like the other fishermen. I wish Oto-san was home, not me, when the F.B.I. come and they shoot him *ma`ke* die-dead. Then I no find him hanging when I come home from school."

"I hate our father."

They were horrible, traitorous words. "Me, too."

They sat together, not speaking, their bond cemented by the man who always hung in their minds on the end of a rope, grotesque and smelling, his fury and despair as adhesive as love.

CHAPTER FOURTEEN

In which Melba's dead mother visits the hospital again and a veil is pierced

Mama. It's you. Though clouds conceal you, I would know you anywhere. You come alone, gowned and cool. Is it for me that you come? At last? You pause. I hesitate in response and the distance is never bridged. We can never return to our original closeness, me resting inside you, curled and unknown, draining your blood, leaching your teeth and bones while you wash rice and mend and wonder calmly who I am.

A pink light the color of lotus in the evening poured around the evanescent figure who stood very still but seemed at the same time to tremble like the smallest leaf at the tip of the newest spring limb, luminous, and blessed. Kimono sleeves fluttered. The pink of her mother's garment was a softer hue of the rosy light, and disappeared into it, leaving the edges transparent. Melba recognized with gladness the pale silk with its delicate wisteria embroidery, and moved shyly forward. Her mother's jet-black hair was upswept and pricked with silver flowers. Her face, as Melba approached, was young and impassive. She was dressed as Melba remembered, for the Obon, the Dance of the Dead, when the taiko drums at Hongwanji thundered and lanterns were sent out on the evening tides to guide souls home.

Is there no lantern for me, Mama? I cared for you until the end and you bring no light. I hear no drum. Your hands are hidden. I am, once more, up against your powerful silence. All my struggles were always with you, weren't they? I thought Oto-san was my problem, what he did, how I found him. I was wrong. Fathers can do terrible things that injure us, but it is how our mothers defend us, or don't; how they react to what has been done to us, that defines our gravity.

It's not fair. Every woman would shrink from motherhood at all costs if she truly understood it. But we are deceived by love again, the hot breath of passion swooning about our throat, then a tiny hand fiercely curled around our finger, a mouth sucking our milk.

It is too daunting to contemplate that every maternal gesture is critical, every word, every missed opportunity, every tired evening when weariness sweaters love in wooly indifference while a child stands radiantly on the brink of expectation. Words said carelessly, thoughtlessly echo in the blood, poisoning the heart. A tone of voice, the exact nuance of injury, is remembered for a lifetime. A mother's glance can still wither when the child is forty. What do we do, Mama, as mothers?

Once we were goddesses. Ancient clay women, round in the belly, unearthed from the ashes of dawn, bear witness to this truth. Our mysteries were shrouded in moon cycles, blood and incantations. Helpless men fell down before us, devotees of our power, their hands bloody from hunting our food, while we ate and grew ponderous with new tribes.

Now mothers are an inconvenience. We are persuaded to take medication to dam our powers, to even rip the life from inside our bodies. Instead of homage and burnt offerings mothers now receive a begrudged monthly check when the law insists. All the generations that came through you to me, and from me to my daughter, all the survival that led to us, is blocked by the little pill my daughter swallows so eagerly.

Melba saw tears in her mother's eyes. They glistened like the silver flowers in her hair.

Love looks at us through tears. Motherhood is a sacrificial role. My life is required, not in a gush of blood on an altar of stone, but surrendered or stolen in small segments, sometimes twenty minutes at a time. And even the sacrifice, without love, fails. A mother who does not fall to her knees nightly in terror and pleading with the divine, prostrate before her own inadequacies and responsibilities, is a dangerous mother. She may raise monsters.

Mama, you gave us love, you sacrificed your whole life for your children. And still, we hungered for more, for what was beyond you to give. Is that why you have come now? To lead me to that feast which will finally fill me?

Melba wanted to rush into her mother's arms and be enveloped but those arms moved abruptly from the kimono sleeves, straight out, palms facing Melba as two walls of flame.

Melba stopped. While she watched, her mother turned her back and was consumed in a blush of light and the light faded.

It was night. She felt the weight of the tucked blanket over her feet. A nurse withdrew, dimming the light. Melba was positive that just for that moment, that brief moment that passed before she could move or speak, she crossed back into the world of hospital bed and pain, and she was so happy her heart smiled within. She remembered her mother's visit, the fragrance of incense and green tea that surrounded her. The implied invitation.

CHAPTER FIFTEEN

Featuring the atomic bomb and sixteen kinds of
ants

"FIRE BOMBS BLAST JAPS
RAIDS CRIPPLE NIP INDUSTRY"
It was August 6, 1945 and that was the headline
of the *Honolulu Advertiser*. Those were the words in big
bold type that trumpeted the dreadful news into the little
green shack in the back of the banana farm in Manoa
Valley. It was evening and Raymond had brought the
newspaper home. He was breathless from running and
his eyes betrayed a lurid excitement. "It's a new kind of
bomb," he said, glancing around the room, demanding
by his palpable and unusual wildness, complete
attention. "Listen to this." He read, obviously having
read every word before. "'What is the Atomic Bomb? It
is the most terrifying engine of destruction ever devised
by man, according to press reports. It has the explosive
force of 20,000 tons of TNT. Its use against Japan was
announced yesterday by President Truman.'"

Raymond looked up from the newspaper. "Wow.
Twenty thousand tons of TNT on Hiroshima." The
newspaper was an emblem of Raymond's status as part-

time grocery clerk. He had gone looking for a job after
Peter was inducted into the army. He turned his small
wages and tips over to Mama and he got to bring a
newspaper home if there was one left at closing time.

Melba, Hazel and Avis gathered around him on
the floor to look at the paper. At fifteen years old,
Melba's emotions were like the sudden storms that
gather against the Ko`olau peaks, dump torrents of rain
and move on out over the ocean, trailing rainbows. The
twins had grown into spiders, all arms and legs, long
black hair hitched behind their ears, their movements as
unpredictable as Melba's moods. Their mother sat in the
room's only chair, mending a dress. If she understood
what Raymond read, she showed no reaction. If Peter
was not in the army but home and doing the reading, she
would have tried to understand She continued to reweave
the underarm of the dress.

Melba had never seen Raymond so agitated. It
was as if he had something hot in his hand and didn't
know where to drop it. He spoke words that were evil,
unaware of their power because they were paper,
because they were someone else's and not his own. He
made her nervous. She looked to their mother, whose
head was bent over her task, then looked out the
window. The moon was ice and all around it was pure
radiance.

Raymond continued, breathing life into the bomb, "It's a new secret weapon."

"No more secret now," Avis said, "The Japonese know all about it. They wen get it good."

Hazel asked, "If we beat the Japonese, then the army let Peter come home from Michigan?"

Her twin, the practical one, answered, "Maybe not right away. They gotta mop up."

"What happens if the Japonese get one atomic bomb li' dat?"

"They don't have or they drop one on us at Pearl Harbor." Avis glanced at her mother, then lowered her voice to a whisper, "Where Mama's family come from? Near da bomb?"

Raymond answered, "Nagasaki. Don't worry, it's not even on the same island as Hiroshima."

Their mother concentrated on the dress as if her life depended on it.

Melba, sideways to the paper, read about ship sinkings and unconfirmed reports of massive destruction in Hiroshima. The print went uphill toward Raymond's hand. When she turned to the window again, the moon was gone, the sky black. The phrase, "the most terrifying engine of destruction ever devised by man," fascinated her. She was ashamed to be so intrigued. She might not have been ashamed if the moon hadn't hidden its face at that exact moment. When she went to sleep that night, the words waltzed in her head like a catchy tune, "the most terrifying engine of destruction ..."

The next evening, Raymond again brought home a newspaper. It proclaimed in thick black type:

"NEW ATOM RAID HINTED"

He read aloud: "Japan conceded today that 'new type bombs' caused 'considerable damage' yesterday in Hiroshima."

Melba read that reconnaissance planes were still unable to penetrate the smoke over the city. She remembered the black puffs in the sky over Honolulu when Pearl Harbor was bombed, how the sun kept shining and the flowers kept blooming while three thousand people were dying. She imagined the people in Hiroshima looking up into a sky full of smoke, all their flowers burned, wondering if the sun would ever shine again, if the moon was still in place.

Raymond said, "Listen to this – a sailor said to President Truman, 'Send some more of 'em over Japan and we'll all go home.' The president was having lunch on a ship." Raymond straightened a wrinkle in the paper, then read in a school voice: "Mr. Truman said afterward that he had never been happier about any announcement he had made. 'The experiment has been an overwhelming success.'"

Hazel read another page-one headline: "Punahou Youth Takes Stock, and Puts Ban on Sloppy Dress."

Avis asked, "What the rich kids worried about? The maid no iron their underwear?"

Melba was impatient, "It says they're going to have a school dress code. It says 'no more shirt tails fanning the breeze, no more dirty dungarees or bandanas.' Why they put this kine stuff on page one with the atom bomb? Like the Punahou kids' dirty dungarees the same ting as the most terrible engine of destruction ever devised by man get dropped on Japan."

Hazel read, "Sixteen Kinds of Ants and Honolulu Has 'Em All." She looked at Melba triumphantly. "It says it right here. A whole story on ants right unnerneat the atomic bomb."

Melba slapped the paper to the floor and went outside. She sat on the steps, wanting to cry. She couldn't explain it. After a few minutes her mother came out and sat beside her, so close their clothes touched. Melba felt hot. She sprang up and walked over to the outdoor sink, "It's okay, Mama. I just washing my face." She cupped the cold water to her eyes. How could she tell her mother how she felt when they had so few words between them?

She wanted to shake her mother and ask, "Where are your feelings? What goes on inside your head? Your

heart has grown so small it's a wonder you can move
your eyelids without having a stroke. I never want that to
happen to me. I want to live life to the fullest. I want to
understand and know. Why are people so filled with hate
instead of love? I want to know about the most terrible
engine of destruction, what it means. Will an enemy
again fly over Pearl Harbor some day and this time the
smoke will be so thick that the sun will not shine and the
moon over the Ko`olau will break apart? And everyone
on the island will die. I do not consent to this.

Melba's indignation and fear electrified her.
Tears poured down her face. She walked about the yard
sniffling until she felt tired and foolish. Everyone came
out on the steps. Their faces were blue and incandescent
as they pretended to watch the moon and stars. Melba
stomped up the steps, right through them and slammed
the screen door. She didn't know what to make of
herself.

The news continued to get worse. On August
eighth, the *Advertiser* headline announced: "Tokyo Says:
When Bomb Hit ALL LIFE PERISHED."

Raymond read aloud, "One hundred thousand
may have died in holocaust."

Melba put her hands over her ears. A hundred
thousand what? Ants? One hundred thousand mothers,
fathers, brothers, sisters, children, babies, alive one

minute and dead the next, their ghosts stunned and
babbling.

Raymond stopped reading, watching her with her
ears covered.

She realized how overwrought and dramatic the
gesture was and become embarrassed. She told him, "It's
okay. You can read.'

He shrugged, "No need. All the same."

On August ninth Raymond came running home
early. Out of breath, he leaned against a young *kukui* tree
on the edge of the clearing. Hazel and Avis were
weeding the vegetable garden. He asked, "Mama home?"

"No," they chorused.

"Try get Melba."

Hazel ran.

Melba was already coming down the steps,
wiping her hands on her rice bag apron.

Raymond showed her the *Advertiser* headline:
"NAGASAKI IS BLASTED OFF MAP BY ATOM
BOMB."

She sat down in the grass; the breath gone out
from her.

The twins imitated her shock, glad to have a
break from the weeding. They looked at each other and
curled their bony shoulders inward.

Raymond said, "We better go meet Mama, in

case she knows."

They took an unlit lantern and matches in case she was late. They went all the way to the bus stop without meeting her. The sun was going down beyond Waikiki, a huge fireball of molten pink and orange, larger and more flamboyant than usual. Beyond it was Japan … burning.

Melba asked, "You think the atomic bomb look li' dat sun?"

Raymond answered, "I think it has no color. I think it's so bright it absorbs all color, worse than the sun in the middle of the day." He adjusted his new glasses on the bridge of his nose. He looked scholarly. He opened his newspaper, "Listen to the editorial. It says, 'The world stands upon the threshold of a new era of greater enlightenment or of approaching darkness.'"

Hazel asked, "Can someone drop the atomic bomb on us?"

Raymond paused. "No one else has the atomic bomb, so we're safe."

She hunched up against him, "For now. Till someone else figure it out. By den we be boring grown-ups and no care if we ma-ke or not."

Avis asked, "If all those people in Nagasaki dead, and all their kids dead, and their grandkids and cousins dead, who get their stuff?"

Melba answered impatiently, "What stuff? There's nothing left. Everything is burned to a crisp."

"Then who gets the ground? Maybe Mama."

They saw the bus down the road. Raymond warned, "Don't ask Mama questions like that. Okay?"

Avis pouted, "I was just wondering. Maybe we rich. Maybe no more live in Uncle Hideshi's shack."

Raymond warned again, with just a glance.

Their mother was the only one left on the bus. As she got off, Melba noticed her step was unsteady as her black shoe touched the ground. There was no color in her face, as if she had seen the very face of the atom bomb and it had sucked her dry. Her eyes burned like coals. She did not acknowledge the presence of her children, but in crippling silence, marched past them and started up the road in the approaching darkness. They scrambled after her, not quite sure they had done the right thing coming to meet her.

Raymond lit the lantern when they reached the trail head while their mother bent and carefully removed her leather shoes. He tried to walk close behind her, to light her path. She stopped, annoyed by his closeness, his hovering, and motioned for him to go ahead, shooing him like a dog. She stood aside and grunted at Melba and the twins to also go past her. She let them get a few feet ahead, then walked behind them, by herself, emanating an anger so tremendous it burned their backs. The twins stumbled. Melba felt awkward and inadequate.

In words somewhere between a growl and a whisper, between fury and compassion, Raymond said over his shoulder, "I wish I was Peter. Then Mama might be consoled."

Melba knew he was right and wanted to throw mud at their mother who was so dry and brittle and hard, any hand that touched her would come away with splinters, any heart that pitied her was in danger of infection. Melba said, "I'm glad you're Raymond."

When they got to Auntie Junko's house, Mama told them to go on home. She would come later. Melba knew they had failed her, as they failed their father. They were not enough.

Mama did not come home until morning when the birds were singing wildly in the trees and the leaves of the banana trees waved stiffly against each other. Mama had powdered her face, but Melba saw she had cried, maybe all night. Perhaps there was some hope for her heart.

CHAPTER SIXTEEN

In which Sweetie visits The Mango Queen in the hospital and threatens to give her cherry red hooker nails.

A friend is a guest in your life, someone who comes and stays, but is free to leave at any moment. She carries nothing of the messy bondage of blood or law or doctrine. She is a volunteer.

Sweetie, I know you're here, and I wish I could tell you how much I have always loved you, but, as you can see, I cannot speak, and even if I could, I probably wouldn't say it. I wouldn't even send a Thinking-of-You card with bluebirds on it. No need. You know.

Sweetie held Melba's hand, giving her a manicure. She had a bowl of lemon water in which she soaked the limp fingers, then eased away the cuticles. Her movements were so naturally graceful, she looked more like she was playing a violin than leaning over a hospital bed doing an invalid's nails. Her thick black hair was brushed softly back from her remarkably unlined face in a neatly pinned tumble of curls anchored with a gardenia.

As she pulled gently on Melba's softened skin, revealing first one pink half-moon and then another, she talked, "Now Melba, if you don't snap out of this coma, I'm going to come in tomorrow and paint your nails blood red -- the color you always hated on me – Very Cherry. You know I'll do it. And you'll be lying here with ten slutty red nails when your family, who don't know your true nature like I do, come in. Then you'll have to wake up just to issue denials. This clear polish I'm putting on today is only an undercoat. Tomorrow -- Vampira. Unless, of course, you open your eyes right this minute and tell me you want a nice ladylike pink."

Melba felt the strength and authority in her friend's touch, and the casual warmth that came from years of long phone calls. *I know I'm alive when someone touches me. Friendship. What is this thing? It's so porous anything can pass through it. It's lovely and usually transient as clouds are to the sky -- and just as definitive and dangerous, as full of illusions and thunder. But never deadly, because it is separate from you. A friend not only allows you to keep your apartness, she celebrates it with you. She likes you because of who you are, not because of who you can become with a little guidance and weight loss. A friend does not expect you to fill in missing parts of herself. She has no power over you. Yes, a friend can wound, but it's never mortal, as a lover's or parent's knife can be. That's why friends are so safe.*

Sweetie, I remember how you found that scraggly mango tree in the forest when I was so wretched, living in the back of my uncle's banana farm, how you made everything so happy and fragrant when you came to the house, if I can be so generous as to call that shack a house.

Sweetie kept talking as she filed first one nail, and then another. "Oh, Melba, you were wild. We both were, but you -- you were way out there. If our kids only knew, yah? We lived on rum and Coca-Cola, and foot-long hot dogs from Donald Duck Drive-In. Those were the days -- dancing in Waikiki every night. All those soldiers on the way to Korea. Hooo – some of the jerks we met, I tell you, Girl. And I married one. No, just kidding. I dearly love Hal, but he's sure no party animal anymore. He is in low gear, parking his *okole* in the Lazy Boy. I check his pulse every once in a while. If the Lazy Boy had a built-in cooler and a *lua* – that man would never move." She examined a fingernail for symmetry. "Hal talked to Dick Bower over the weekend. Remember I told you Dick's wife had colon cancer? Well, she *ma-ke* poor ting. And Melba, I don't know how you feel about this, but Hal invited Dick Bower to come to Hawai'i. I promise I had nothing to do with it. I thought Hal should go there, to Florida, you know, for the funeral. But the Lazy Boy no fly. So, Dick is coming here to visit. Hal told him about you and your accident, and he's all concerned." She rounded the sharp edges of a clipped nail.

Wait. Melba could not register her alarm, which made it more frightening. *Stop. Sweetie. You can't bring him here. He can't see me like this.* Melba wanted to claw her way through the psychic scrim separating her from Sweetie, but it was strong, like an airplane window.

Placidly, Sweetie talked as she worked on the nails, as if she had not just delivered catastrophic news. "Do you ever wonder about what your life would be like if you married Dick Bower? You'd be living in Florida running a bird park, maybe teaching those parrots to scream, 'Tora, tora, tora.' That would have been nice, hum? It's not too late, you know. But, Hal says Dick sold his birds. Broke the guy's heart even though the business was on the skids for a while. He can't compete with Disney World. Like which would you rather see if you went to Florida – Disney World or Bower's Amazing Amazon Bird Park? Dick tried everything – he put in a maze, he bribed tour bus drivers, he got one of those colored fountains. He put his parrots on roller skates, bikes, high wires, umbrellas, fire trucks. We saw them when we were there years ago. Those birds were so smart, they could count to ten, play dead, ring bells. Smarter than most of the guys we ran around with, I tell you. But they weren't Mickey and Donald. A mortal just can't compete with gods. I think, for Americans, Mickey Mouse is a little *aumakua*, a guardian spirit helping them along in the hot pursuit of happiness." She finished another nail, examined it. "But all we find when we get to Disney heaven is more stuff to buy. Personally, I believe happiness is either inside you or it's nowhere. You know, I still have that photo of you and Dick by the Edgewater Hotel pool. Do you still have yours? I almost brought it today -- the one where you have the mangoes stuffed into your bathing suit, posing -- and those cat's-eye glasses; they're coming back in now. Oh, those were the days. Dick was so nuts about you. He thought you walked on water. You guys were so perfect."

Dick Bower. Melba rushed away.

CHAPTER SEVENTEEN

In which Melba recalls falling in love with a soldier who goes away.

The moon was almost full, exceptionally large and bright as it rose. It turned the sluggish Ala Wai into molten silver and gave it riverine aspirations. It was the kind of moon that encouraged fleeting and startling speculation in even the most self-centered and youthful of observers about the minuteness of one's place in the scheme of the universe. Melba and Sweetie paused on the McCully Street Bridge and looked up into the sky at the huge cloud-torn halo around the moon and saw the feathery silver-on-silver embossing of lunar canyons.

"Mahina o hoku," Sweetie said. "The moon of the star. My Papa Nui plants his sweet potatoes on nights like this. Once in a while when we go country, I help him. I love the sound of the *'o'o* entering the earth, and the dirt giving way -- it fills up the whole world. We never talk. I know he prays while he plants, with his back bent and his hands in the soil. Great blessings and abundance come from all you do under *mahina o hoku*. Then when the sky starts to get light, my Mama Nui makes rice and Portuguese sausage and we smell it from

the field and I get so hungry and the hunger feels so good I almost don't want to go in to eat. I'd rather be out there in the quiet and the prayers. I love the night."

"Don't you do a song like that?"

"About Portugese sausage?"

"No, Silly. *Mahina o hoku.* Who sings about sausage?"

"Auhea wale oe..." Sweetie began to sing and sway, her right hand extended over the water. She stopped abruptly. "Maybe we'll meet our Prince Charmings tonight." Her face radiated health. Her smooth and buttery body seemed poured into her spaghetti-strap dress that fluttered in the breeze from the Ala Wai and melded with the moon's light path on the water. "Don't you wish you could see your future?" she asked.

"I do see my future, and if I think about it, I'll jump off this bridge." Melba's beauty was more sultry than her friend's, though she was dressed in a gathered purple skirt and a modest purple and white striped blouse with silk violets pinned at the throat. There was something smoldering, repressed and sad about her that was immensely appealing.

"Melba, don't even joke like that. I mean I'd never commit suicide, no matter what. I'm just too *niele*. I want to see how my life turns out, good or bad. And yours and everyone's. I want to see what cars will look like ten years from now and whether we'll get to walk on that big old moon in our lifetime and whether there are little green men on Mars. The big things. If you jump ..."

Melba knew Sweetie was about to say more, but remembered Oto-san. Instead, Sweetie offered her a cigarette. They both lit up and leaned over the concrete bridge railing, inhaling with great pleasure and absently watching the silver Ala Wai slink beneath them with a Sunday languor.

Sweetie asked, "You hear from Shuzo?"

"Is the world round? Of course I heard from Shuzo. I swear he writes every day. Every day the same thing – he's freezing and he misses me. Alaska most be a real drag -- at least to him." She unconsciously shivered.

"Hoo, you've got sympathy chills, girl. That's a sign. You're connected."

"Thinking about him gives me the chills, as in the willies. I mean, Shuzo's a nice guy. Really nice, but such a square. If I marry him, I can just see my whole life -- living in his mother's nice little house in Kaimuki, a bunch of kids, boring, boring, boring -- never go anywhere. I have dreams, Sweetie. I want to leave this island someday."

"For good?"

"I don't know. Maybe. I dream about it."

"Look at Shuzo. He's off the island and I bet he wishes he was right back here this very minute."

"That's my whole point. If I was in Alaska, I'd be hugging polar bears and going ice skating and wearing nice fur coats. I'd make the most of it. He hates it."

"Then let's make the most of this minute, this night. Look at us. We are the cat's meow, Melba."

They laughed. Sweetie added, "And you should fall down on your knees every night thanking your lucky stars the army sent Shuzo to Alaska and not Korea, like the poor joes we meet all the time."

"Yeah. He wouldn't last two minutes in Korea. Knowing him, he'd jump in front a bullet to save someone else. Blam. No more Shuzo."

"Yeah. Poor Shuzo. You know, I met this great guy last week when you couldn't come. I hope I hope he's there tonight." Sweetie spun around. "Hal Adkins, a doll, a living doll."

"Maybe he has a friend."

"He does. But I think the guy likes Millie."

"I told my mother I was staying at your house. If she ever knew I was going to USO dances she'd kill me. *Ma-ke.*"

"There's always room at our house," Sweetie said, "on the sofa, on the sleep porch, under the piano."

"There's always a party at your house." They began to walk. Melba asked, "Millie them coming tonight?"

"We're meeting them at USO. I always like to be just a little late, you know, make a grand entrance, music playing."

Melba held out her skirt, "Tah-dah." She took one last pull on her cigarette and flicked it in the Ala Wai, "This is going to be a wonderful, wonderful night. I can feel it, can't you?" She paused, shrugged. "Of course, the last time I felt like this, like something really big was going to happen, Oahu got bombed."

Sweetie nudged her friend, "Just don't you get bombed tonight."

"You're a fine one to talk."

"Yeah, but I don't sneeze all over the place and get sick."

"Don't worry. I can take care of myself." Melba thrust her chin in the air, dangerously optimistic. "Tonight, Sweetie, we are the cat's meow." They drifted toward Fort DeRussy, on the *ewa* edge of Waikiki. The air was so soft and fragrant with plumeria that when a breeze touched their skin, it was like a caress. It was all they knew of sensuality.

Melba continued, "Let's not get contaminated by squares. If Millie brings her friend Catherine what's-her-name, with the yo-yo glasses and flat hair, let's steer clear."

Sweetie protested, "Catherine's nice."

"Catherine is mosquito repellant -- only for guys." Melba's tone was light and cruel.

They walked through the lobby of the USO, elaborately not noticing the young soldiers and sailors whose heads snapped around in their direction. They paused for effect at the entrance to the dance hall. The band had just finished playing a fast song and everyone was perspiring and wiping. The failures were being ushered back to the sidelines.

Melba and Sweetie gazed upon the dance floor. They stood poised, cool, and they knew they were beautiful. Melba surveyed the room and dismissed it even though she believed destiny would somehow reveal itself that evening. She wouldn't even have to look for it. Her fate would find her.

Sweetie anxiously searched the sea of faces for Hal Adkins and tried not to look disappointed when she didn't see him. "Look, there's Millie folks," she said, rising on the balls of her feet.

Millie waved, motioning them over.

"She's with Lani, Caroline, Lei Anne -- and Catherine," Melba said, "Let's take the long way over, go around the room. Maybe we'll get lucky and be rescued on the way." The band launched into, "Mona Lisa." The singer, a sailor, did a credible imitation of Nat King Cole. The girls were almost to their friends' table when a soldier tapped Sweetie on the shoulder from behind.

She whirled around, and happiness broke out in every aspect of her almond face, the way the sun rises from the ocean in the morning and suddenly all the light is gold. Coyly, she tempered her enthusiasm, "Oh, hi." Casual, but not too casual. "You're the guy I met last week -- from Ohio, right? Hal Adkins, right?"

Sweetie was so smooth. She glanced happily over her shoulder at Melba as she was whisked onto the dance floor. And there, standing right behind where Hal had been, was destiny in a uniform. The recognition was instantaneous and Melba was too shocked, too thrilled to even smile. There was a maturity about this one, his stance, even his body, which was filled out and solid, not wasp-waisted and hesitant. His face was smooth, his hair brown, his eyes blue and much too confident. It was easy to see he was pleased at the sight of her and that he was accustomed to having his way. She pictured him riding a motorcycle. He moved with leonine confidence toward Melba, his arms already in the dance position, assuming she would slip into them, and she did. He pulled her close, his mouth immediately in her hair. She heard him sigh and wondered if it was a strategy   She leaned away slightly and said, "Our friends left us without even introducing us."

He gently pulled her close again, "Who needs an introduction?"

Melba settled into his shape, pleased at how they were so naturally in step. She hoped he couldn't feel her heart beating, betraying.

After a minute, he whispered, "I'll just call you Mona Lisa."

"Then I'll call you Leonardo."

He straightened up, pulled back, suddenly stiff and looked down at her, "That's a grease ball name if I ever heard one."

Melba knew she had irritated him, and was surprised at the suddenness and candor of his reaction. In her best and cheeriest voice, she said, "That's who painted the Mona Lisa, Leonardo DaVinci." Nervously, she offered further amelioration, "One of the greatest artists of all time. Mona Lisa was his mystery woman." She tried harder, "You can tell when you look at her face, that they went all the way." She was not about to lose this soldier, and watch her fate slip through her fingers. "I'll be your mystery woman. You will never know my name. You may beg, but my lips are sealed."

He grinned down at her, nodding his head,

knowing her game, the stakes she moved onto the table. "My Mona Lisa." He turned her, pulled her close, kissed the top of her ear. The music stopped. They made no move to leave the floor.

Hal and Sweetie came over, holding hands, about to burst. "Well," Sweetie said, rocking back on her heels slightly, brushing Hal's chest, "You two obviously need no introduction." Sweetie turned to Hal and said, "This is my best friend in the whole world, Melba Yamada."

Melba glanced at Hal and thought he must have hollow bones, like a bird. He was tall and loosely jointed, seemingly composed as much of air as matter. "Pleased to meet you." To each his own.

In her excitement, Sweetie was missing all the clues, the nuances in the demeanor of her friend. She practically babbled. "Dick, you're Dick Bower. I met you last week. You're from Indiana, right?"

"Last time I looked."

"See I remember everything."

Melba did not dare to glance at Dick, afraid he'd see she was on fire, raging. She stared modestly down at her sandals.

The next song was "Because of You." Dick Bower took her hand and they slid right into the music without another word or glance at their friends, as if no one else existed. Dick squeezed her about the waist,

"Melba, Melba, Melba. Now I know your name. Will you still be my mystery Mona Lisa?"

Over his khaki shoulder Melba saw Millie look longingly at Dick. "Um hum," she said with great smugness. She knew where she was going. Dick Bower's touch electrified her. She had never felt this way before. She tingled in mysterious places. They danced every dance.

At the end of the evening, as the band played, "Good night, Sweetheart," he said, "I can't say goodnight to you."

"Me, too."

"We can walk on the beach."

"Um hum. The moon is beautiful tonight. *Mahina o hoku*, the moon of the star."

"That's beautiful." He hesitated. "I -um - Hal and I have a room at the Edgewater. He and Sweetie are going up to Queen's Surf to dance some more after this. We can go with them, or, um, we can go to the room, have a few drinks, get to know each other."

She felt the beat of his heart racing ahead of the flow of his words and was suddenly confident, having ascertained her position in the balance of power. She whispered, "I'm thirsty. Drinks sound good." They danced close, arms wrapped around each other. She was startled to feel his arousal. She would lose her virginity this evening. She wished she had lost it already. She was overwhelmed with a hunger and urgency that shredded every constraint ever placed upon her.

So, this is it. This is why we risk all. This decision that once made becomes compulsion, a speeding car, a freedom that is delirium and wild, wild abandon.

For the first time, Melba didn't know how her life would turn out, and it was exhilarating.

CHAPTER 18

While Sweetie gives her a manicure, Melba
revisits a long-ago medical emergency.

Melba heard Sweetie's nail file scraping, felt it
become quicker, sharper, perhaps drawing blood.
Yesterday she gave her a manicure. Today apparently it
was a pedicure.

*Sweetie, I know what you're remembering. We
always get just so far talking about Dick Bower, and
then we stop at the abyss of that day. All our fun, our
drinking, all the laughter and music always leads right
to that reeking staircase in Chinatown. The stink of
vomit, urine and ether still fill my nose.*

*I think you were more scared than me. You
thought I was wrong to do it, but you held my hand. I
will never forget that. I had no fear as I climbed those
stairs, because you were there. I was on fire to kill
something -- my own body would have done nicely. I was
so angry I wanted to throw something at the sky and
crack it open. I wanted to maim everyone who had ever
hurt me, starting with my father. I sat in that dingy room
on the chair with the cracked plastic seat, and I don't
know what you were thinking about, but I concentrated*

183

on every injustice, every outrage I could think of. The atom bomb, finding my father hanging from the ceiling fan, my mother pushing Shuzo at me, Shuzo's infuriating decency, even Dick's sweaty love-making, the direct result of which brought me to that disgusting room.

I can still see that scraggly woman, not her face, but the darkness of her clothes, the economy of her movements. When she opened the door to that other room and all the smells of medicine and despair came seeping out, I almost changed my mind. Then the woman asked, "Which one?" and you gasped. I turned around and saw the fear and pleading in your eyes, you half way out of the chair wanting to hold on to me, and I was like an emperor. I could do anything. I held the power of life and death in my hands. And I could hurt even you, my dearest friend, my hoaaloha, the dearest friend of a lifetime. And I liked it. Am I some kind of monster?

I walked in there like one hard-hearted Hannah and handed them the money Dick had left when he shipped out. "Hang onto it, Babe," he told me, "It's our honeymoon fund." But Dick hadn't met my mother. It wasn't until they told me to undress and handed me the white gown, and I looked down at my bare stomach breathing in and out as I slipped off my panties – all of a sudden it was like someone had stabbed me right there. I could hardly straighten up. By the time I got on the table

I was shaking so much my body was actually bouncing on the table. I couldn't stop myself. So, they put a blanket over me. No more courage. Just another pathetic knocked-up kid. Nobody said one word to me. They talked to each other like I was a piece of meat on a slab. The only time the doctor spoke was when he lowered the mask. "Breathe deeply. Count backwards from ten." I gulped that stuff like there was no tomorrow. For one of us, there wasn't.

There was a kind of reckless vengeance about the whole thing, but it was the fury of a tied-up dog that's being beaten by someone just out of reach. That's why I was so shocked by how I felt afterwards. It was like there was a hole inside my body, like a forest that has been cleared to build stores, like a place in the night sky after a star has fallen. It hurt so badly. Not in my body, but in a deeper place, where I am a woman. Simply that -- the elementary defining factor of my walk in this world -- female. And the next day I got up and went to my UH classes and came home and cooked the supper, like nothing had happened, and all day long I kept seeing pregnant women, on the bus, on the sidewalk, in the store. I didn't know there could be so many pregnant women, and each one was a reprimand that got me angrier and angrier until, by the end of the day, I was okay.

Sweetie uncovered Melba's right foot, stroked the skin. "I can just see ten Very Cherry Waikiki-hooker nails -- tomorrow, Melba." She laid out her dish of lemon water, her files and clear polish, her tender threats, and began to work. The window was behind her and, like a tree, Sweetie cast sheltering shade on the bed, cooling the heat of the terrible truths. She said, "Dear Melba, I'm going to sing you something Japanese. Maybe you'll come back to us. I had to learn Japanese songs for my show. The Hawaiian Regent is so full of Japanese tourists, you'd think you were in downtown Tokyo except everyone's wearing new aloha clothes that are too big for them. They look like orphans someone has dolled up for an excursion, complete with name tags. But they're so nice and polite, until the men have a few beers under their belts and then they want you to sing, *Kokoni Sachiari* … enough Hawaiian awreddy." Very softly, in her clear rich voice, Sweetie began to sing, *"Arashi mo fuke ba..."*

Gratefully, on the sails of the song, Melba allowed a flood of memories of Japan to wash over her. She relaxed into remembered smells of green tea, incense and cedar. She saw in her mind the temple in Kamakura, the way sunlight stole softly through bamboo. She inhaled again the tendrils of incense curling from a hundred joss sticks, heard the crunch of gravel just outside the main pagoda, and then she beheld, in all its subdued splendor, the dim golden Buddha, sitting upon smoke, richness glowing around him, so pervasive, so insinuating, she couldn't be sure if the Buddha was there in front of her, or within her.

Sweetie, I need to tell you something.

Her friend was oblivious, absorbed in the pedicure. Her song drifted away into contented humming. Melba began to sob, but she did not shake nor were there tears.

Oh, Sweetie, when I took Mama back to Japan before she died – remember? Ten years ago? Peter paid for the trip. Of course, he didn't go. He was too busy. "You go, Melba. Take Mama. I'll pay for everything." She wouldn't go to Nagasaki. I wanted to see it, but she was firm, and you know her. So, we went to Beppu for the hot springs, and of course Tokyo. The big thing I wanted to do, aside from Nagasaki, was go to Kamakura and see the Daibutsu – that huge Buddha, the one on all the postcards? So off we go one morning on the bullet train out of Tokyo. Well, it turns out Kamakura is full of temples. And it wasn't the big Buddha that spoke to me, even though I paid my yen and walked into his bronze belly. So many tourists must give him indigestion. I posed Mama in front of him. I have never seen her so contented. She actually enjoyed herself.

We had a little map and we were doing the temple trail, stopping in tea houses along the way. One of the temples we visited was Hasedera. They had these beautiful gardens and a view of the bay. And then, off to the side of the main pagoda, we saw a whole hillside of little stone statues of Jizu, the patron of children, the one who guides them from this life to the next. The statues were wearing bibs and bonnets and had little plastic pinwheels and baby rattles and little stuffed toys bundled around them. There were hundreds of them, set out in tiers. We didn't know what they meant, so Mama asked the priest. He told her that each statue represented an aborted or miscarried child. He said that even though abortion is legal and common in Japan, women who have an abortion feel a need for spiritual reconciliation. They need to acknowledge that there was a life, a child. So, they come quietly, usually alone, to Kamakura and they buy a little stone statue and leave it on the hillside with pretty pinwheels spinning in the breeze. The priest said there are so many, that he regularly has older statues cleared to make room for more. The women come by the thousands to kneel and be purified and blessed. That's what he said.

Sweetie, I think Mama knew about the abortion, because right in front of me, she asked the priest what Buddhism teaches about abortion. I felt like it was

*yesterday that same stab in the stomach I had as I
undressed in Chinatown that day. And then the priest
said that the ideal of Buddhism is to kill nothing, to take
no life, not an animal, not an insect, no life at all. He
sounded just like you, Sweetie. Then Mama said she was
going to use the restroom and have tea on the terrace
and why didn't I stay awhile in the temple. I looked at all
those statues in baby clothes, and I was overwhelmed
with sorrow, not just for the babies who were never
born, but for the women driven there by our basic
biological role, and by the failure of others to honor it,
to simply help life. I was so overwhelmed, I fell on my
knees before the priest, before the Buddha, and I
couldn't stop crying. In the land of my ancestors, I could
finally weep for my first child. And I felt blessings pour
over me. Imagine. Me. I bought a statue, but I had no
baby clothes with me, no pinwheel. I was unprepared, so
I left my keychain with the little flashlight on it, and a
box of cough drops. That was all I had.*

    *Nobody ever told me, but I know my baby was a
boy. There in Kamakura, before the Buddha, I told my
baby his name was Jiro Bower, Jiro after my father and
Bower for his own father. Yes. I gave him my father's
name. It seemed to make some kind of circle. While I was
kneeling there in clouds of incense with silence around
me, I knew in the core of my being that my baby forgave*

189

me. And my baby led me to understand that I had to forgive my father. But let me tell you, forgiving him was strictly an intellectual decision. I felt no tenderness. It was almost like the decision was torn from me, as if I was giving up something precious, like if I forgave him, it made what he did okay. But once I decided to do it, I felt this blanket of peace come over me. When I walked away from that hillside, I knew my baby was happy because I had spoken his name and claimed him as my own. And I had unbound his grandfather. In front of the Buddha, I held my hands over the incense dish and scooped the smoke into my face and breathed the ashes.

What will happen to us, Sweetie, when we abandon all our rituals? How will we be healed? Where will our anger and self-loathing go? It goes to guns, to drugs.

Mama was waiting for me in the sunshine. She had bought a bento for me and a cup of green tea and we sat there on the temple terrace overlooking the bay, the way a mother and daughter are supposed to. I knew, for the first time since I was a very little child, how much she loved me, and that maternal love sometimes appears cruel.

Sweetie finished the pedicure, and squeezed Melba's feet. "You know, Melba, that Kenji is one sweetheart, no doubt about it, but I don't see him making any big moves to the jewelry store, so I'm bringing Dick Bower to the hospital the minute he gets to Honolulu. Who knows? Maybe he'll be Prince Charming after all, and he'll kiss you and you'll wake up. Or maybe just the shock of hearing his voice will jolt you bolt upright." Sweetie leaned over and kissed her friend on the cheek, "Melba, I'll do anything to get you back."

CHAPTER 19

In which Melba responds to teriyaki steak and a granddaughter's kiss

Birds. Traffic. The music of life. I am not remembering them. In my darkness I hear them.
As a swimmer tossed and lost in a mighty wave, Melba wasn't sure which way was sunlight and air, and which was deep and everlasting silence. But she felt none of the swimmer's panic that leads to lungs filled with liquid. She saw herself as the swimmer, now at the whim of the wave, becoming an object of great grace and beauty, hair streaming, undulating in currents that encircle the planet, carrying the warm breath of the tropics to far and cold islands, allowing palm trees to prosper on the coast of Erin and whales to find their way home to Hawai'i. She was poised on the edge of the moment of greatest danger, when the temptation to surrender to the universe, to float endlessly and become a thread of an impersonal and gossamer vastness was so easy. Just exhale. The lungs are balloons going flat. She saw the beauty on both sides of the moment, breath and death. She chose breath.
Immediately she became awash in worry, no

longer free and floating. *Dick Bower is coming to Honolulu. To the hospital. His wife is dead. He had parrots and children. I know nothing about them. He knows nothing of me, or his son Jiro, enshrined on a hillside in Kamakura with a flashlight and cough drops.*

Melba breathed in spite of herself. She concentrated on the inflation and deflation of her lungs. It calmed her. And her heart warmed to old possibilities. She imagined an embrace erasing the harsh and relentless passing of years, the treason of the many busy seasons when she never even gave Dick Bower a thought.

He will hold me until it seems he is all I ever thought of. But how will our tomorrows look? Every time we look at each other, in frail dearness, a lei of grey about our heads – assuming Dick Bower still has hair – we will mourn the time we didn't have. We will look at each other and see dissolved rapture, and realize only its desiccated remnant. And it's all my fault. We will never be able to live up to the enormous expectations we will have of each other to be the imagined ideal we were once denied, the arms we ran to in our minds, betraying arms of flesh, real and held out to us, arms consigned now to forever being second best.

Someone entered the room. Melba became aware of losing her power to see as if outside herself, becoming

193

again a prisoner of life.

"Hello, Melba."

Kenji. His dear, familiar voice. And is that teriyaki I smell?

He kissed her on the forehead, then eased into the depths of the flatulent chair.

Melba smiled inside her dormant face. She heard fingers fumble with Styrofoam, and a cover pop open. The teriyaki smell leaped into the room. She smelled the mayonnaise on the macaroni salad.

"I stopped at Zippy's for teri plate," Kenji said. "I almost got two, you are such a habit to me."

Is that what I am? Like the morning paper? I can go to Florida, you know, and be Dick Bower's magnificent obsession. I'm not too old to be an obsession, you know, but I'd miss teriyaki chicken. Maybe Dick can move here. One of us would definitely have to move – thousands of miles away from everything familiar – and live in a strange culture, among people not our own. And the other would have to inflate to fill all the empty spaces. Passion, like everything else as we age, becomes a burden.

As she basked in essence of teriyaki perfume Melba realized, reluctantly, that maybe it was too late to be a magnificent obsession.

Too late – these may be the harshest two words

194

*in life. They acknowledge what could have been, what
still could be, but one of us decides it's not worth it. I
know where rashness leads. I already paid that price and
so did my first son.*

*In the end, am I still my mother's daughter?
Look at me, just accepting what life has brought me.
Some people, mostly men, get to write the script for their
lives. Other people are written upon by life, and they
have it easier because they never have to blame
themselves for the inevitable calamities. At this age I get
to make large choices about my life, all over again. Do
you hear that, Kenji? I don't have to wait for your
proposal. You can keep it. Dick Bower is on his way.*

Melba sighed.

Kenji, sitting beside her, noticed the sigh, but did
not call the nurse. He didn't realize how close she was to
the surface, but he was sure, hearing that exhale and the
sweet long inhale, that she would soon be eating juicy
mangoes and doling them out with her meticulous
justice.

He ate his lunch, then neatly closed the box with
the used chopsticks and paper napkin inside, then put it
in the wastebasket. "Next time, it will be 'two teri plates
to go, Melba. Things will be back to normal."

He turned on the television, sat down and dozed
off.

*Television blather. Teriyaki. So, this is how it is.
It is not the voice of loved ones that will guide us back to
life, but a teri plate lunch and familiar television
commercials we remember in our sleep, in our comas.
Oh, please help me. I am almost there. Please, please
help me, Jack in the Box. Lex Brodie. Kenji, wake up.*

Melba heard, just then, the voices of her
grandchildren coming down the hospital hallway and her
heart smiled with excitement. Immediately she became
acutely aware of her afflicted situation and the effect it
might have on the children.

*How can my son do this? Bring his entire family
to see me. They will be horrified. And I am so exposed
and helpless, like a roach in a jar. I cannot pull up the
blanket. I cannot scold or kiss. Kenji, do something.
Hide me. Send them away. Wake up.*

Kenji roused himself to greet Lance, Kathleen
and the children. Rosemary was the first to throw her
arms around him, "Hi, Uncle Kenji." The child averted
her face from the figure on the bed. A commotion of
hugs engulfed the room, then the family stood
awkwardly arrayed around the bed, not knowing what to
say, waiting to see who would take the only two chairs.

*If you can't think of me, Lance, think of your
children. It's not good for them to see me like this. I'm
scaring them. They see what's ahead of them -- if they're*

lucky and don't get mowed down in youth. No one gets out of life alive. There are no survivors.

How do you think it feels to lie here in a hospital bed with youth gathered around, heedless youth anxious to be out in the sunshine, to turn up their dreadful music, to feel the rush of petty and consuming lust, ignorant of their future. A fate like this is so far ahead of them as to be unimaginable. Ah, when I was young and had mangoes stuffed in my bra and a handsome soldier at my side, I never ever dreamed it would come to this, either. And neither do you. We imagine the expedience of nuclear war, tsunami, car wreck or merely our insignificance to save us from incontinence and death. If we lie low, we think, fate will not notice us.

I'm itchy, Lance. I think I'm allergic to Kathleen. She's a good wife, I know that. And a wonderful mother. I can't complain. I never have to worry about my grandchildren the way many other grandmothers do these days, swooping in to rescue the keiki *from negligent, strung-out mothers and their drug-crazed boyfriends. And I see you're happy. But I can't relax around her. I watch my English. I see my house as she sees it. Comfortable but no taste. Old colors -- mustards, olives, browns, the orange shag wall to wall. The spindly legged 1950s coffee table. It never matters except when Kathleen comes around that I don't have one of those*

Berber rugs. Look at her smiling at me and crying. I know those green puddles are genuine, but it makes me angry to be an object of her pity.

"Hi, Mom." Kathleen was the first to take Melba's hand.

Stand back. Let your husband greet his mother first. Haoles *always have to be first. And you don't even see it, it's so natural. You need a class in being second.*

Lance urged his sons forward, "Greet your grandmother." The boys were tall and *hapa* -handsome.

Tiernan pulls more the Oriental side. He graduates Saint Louis this year. Riley – let's see – he's two years younger – that makes him fifteen. He looks more like his mother, square-jawed and careless.

The boys each leaned down and kissed Melba, "Hi Grandma," then retreated to the doorway, probably wondering how long they had to stay and where the cafeteria was.

Rosemary, the child of my heart, it's okay to hang back.

From the day Rosemary was born, Melba insisted she could see herself in the child. The infant had folded her tiny hands across her chest, and with dark eyes contemplated the world, tranquil in the belief that it was good. Now that Rosemary was ten, Melba was even more sure of the resemblance to herself in spite of

Rosemary's red hair.

She is going to be stunning, a heart breaker, with her Asian eyes and golden skin -- and that hair.

Rosemary hesitated, her body curled inward, leaning against her mother, her eyes wide and staring at Melba.

Kathleen urged, "Come on, Honey. It's like Grandma's sleeping but she can't wake up just yet."

The child glanced furtively at the plastic bag of urine dangling from the side of the bed, then quickly turned to examine the wall, embarrassed and frightened.

Her mother encouraged her, "Here, just hold Grandma's hand. If you don't want to kiss her, that's okay."

Rosemary pulled her lips into her mouth, then, having reached a resolution, stepped up to the bed and took her grandmother's bony hand in her own soft one.

It felt so good to Melba, so very good, she wanted to cry. Then Rosemary leaned over and kissed her on the cheek.

My dearest love. My heart is grinning.

Melba's eyes opened. She blinked. *I am seeing again, truly, with my eyes.* Amazed, she turned her head on her pillow, first to one side then the other, and looked all around the room in utter wonder.

Kathleen clasped her hands to her mouth. "Oh

my God."

Tears welled in Lance's eyes, "Mama. You're back." He bent over, embracing his daughter with his body, stroking his mother's head.

Kathleen rushed out for a nurse.

A great flurry of medical personnel descended. They shooed the family out of the room, pulled the curtain around the bed, poked and prodded Melba, listened to her heart, rapped her knee, asked questions – her name, the names of her children, the name of the president of the United States.

Melba wanted a glass of water.

"Sip slowly," a nurse advised

The doctor finished his ministrations and announced, "Mrs. Matsuda, you're going to be fine," as if he, personally, had resurrected her.

Melba thanked him as if, indeed, he had, and asked, "My family can come back in now?"

"The best medicine," he answered. He whipped back the curtain in the manner of a magician pulling off a great stunt, and the family flowed back in, jubilant. This was their personal Easter.

Lance hugged Rosemary. "You had the magic touch."

She answered, "Grandma looked like Sleeping Beauty, sort of, so I kissed her on the cheek. It always works." She beamed, proud and winsome. "At least in fairy tales." Rosemary favored old books with silken pages, lavishly illustrated with tissue pages over the picture pages. She said of modern books, "The colors scream." So, the whole family combed used book stores and religiously attended the Friends of the Library sales. She wanted to be a writer when she grew up.

"Ah," Melba said, "But I'm no beauty. I'm more like the old troll under the bridge."

"*Ka Palapala*," Kenji, almost forgotten in the festivities, reminded her, "And don't you forget it."

Lance added, "You still have it, Mom."

"Where? In my pinkie?" She held up her finger, suddenly overwhelmed with her ability to do so.

Riley and Tiernan stood close to the foot of the bed, awkwardly shifting from foot to foot. Riley said, "We're glad to have you back, Grandma."

"Your hair looks lighter. I hope you're not streaking it, Son."

He ran his fingers through it. He obviously liked the look: "Been surfing."

Tiernan rescued his younger brother from peroxide confessions, "You should see him ride 'em, Grandma. Local Motion may sponsor him – give em all kine jams and t-shirts."

"That's very well and good but you can't earn a

living on a surfboard. You still have to study. You have
to have a profession, Riley."

"Surfing is big time." He was impassioned in
his protest. "The pots are right up there. You can make
good money now as a pro. You never have to buy
clothes. They just give you all this way-cool stuff."

Lance said, "Grandma's right, Riley. Surfing is a
great sport. But you gotta have something else going on.
You gotta have Plan B."

Kathleen's voice was that extra decibel louder,
and always had an unconscious, sharp defensiveness to
it, even when addressing her son. "Think of your poor
mother. When I see those surfers on the news riding the
monster waves at Waimea, all I can think of is -- where's
his poor mother? Neither do I want, God forbid, your
board washing ashore someday with a big shark bite in it
and you nowhere to be found."

Riley grinned and shook his head. He was at the
age when a boy is pleased by a mother's anxiety. It's a
prelude to the games he will play with women for the
rest of his life.

Tiernan knew this. "That's exactly what the kid
wants. Not the shark part, of course, but the big wave
and worried mother scenario. He dreams about riding in
the tube of a forty-footer with the network videos rolling
and Mom screaming her guts out."

Kathleen answered, "Over my dead body." She had a wonderful arsenal of all-occasion last-word flippancies. She turned to her mother-in-law, "Mom, you'll be coming home soon. We'll get your house all ready for you."

Melba panicked – Kathleen cleaning her house. She pictured her daughter-in-law rearranging everything, putting things away where she can't find them, buying a salad spinner and putting it on the kitchen counter. She wanted to snap back "Over my dead body" but it was too close to the truth so she said with sugar on her tongue, "Oh, no need do that. I like things a certain way. And you know how I like to keep busy."

Kathleen turned to Lance, "She needs to keep busy. Will you listen to her? She's flat on her back and she's talking busy. Mom, you're too much. Next thing you'll be back up in the mango tree."

"Has anyone picked the mangoes yet?" Melba asked. "It's time, you know."

Aggrieved, Lance said, "You're back Mom, lining up the chores for everyone. There is such a thing as HPD. The captain expects me to show up for my shift and fight crime. No, the mangoes are not picked. We been spending all our spare time, here, worried about you."

"Staring at a vegetable when you should be

picking fruit."

"Mom, don't even talk that way. We'll get 'um picked. Your job is to get well enough to bake the bread -- or share your recipe."

Now she did say it, "Over my dead body." It is so easy to stop a conversation if you have the right cliche.

Everyone laughed nervously, except Rosemary, who had worry lines creasing her beautiful young brow. "Don't say dead, Grandma. It's like calling it on yourself. I don't like it."

Melba reached for the child's hand. "Bring Grandma some mango tomorrow, will you? A nice juicy one." She closed her eyes. "Tomorrow. What a wonderful word."

CHAPTER 20

The return of the smoothie

Melba showered, shampooed, lavished on sample envelopes of Amirage body lotion (courtesy of Hazel), did up her eyes and blushed her lips. She glanced down at the pink satin bed jacket Sweetie bought for her in happy anticipation of the grand reunion of old lovers. Melba smoothed the lush fabric over her breasts and arranged herself in the bed, wondering if Dick Bower would be shocked at the sight of her. He would probably be expecting the Mango Queen of Waikiki, ageless, reckless, easy – just as she was expecting Private Richard Bower, daring, handsome, funny, twenty. She tried to adjust her image of him, age him with the computer of her mind, and he still came up twenty.

She smiled to herself. We allow the ones we love to see us disheveled, disagreeable, at our worst, yet let an old boyfriend pop up and out come the pots of make-up, the slenderizing dress, the resuscitated charms, so he will writhe in agony over what he missed out on.

Melba heard Sweetie talking full speed as she ushered Hal – and Dick Bower – down the hallway toward her room. Judging by the volume as the little party approached, she knew Sweetie was very nervous, operating at a fever pitch, and that had a calming effect on Melba.

Her friend swept into the room like a garden on the move, orchids in her hair, floral muumuu billowing, arms outstretched, "You look so beautiful, Dear." In the turbulence of her wake, were two *haole* men -- Hal, of course, his eyes taking in everything then settling into disinterest, and the other, a wider, more substantial figure, who had to be Dick Bower wearing the kind of tiki infested aloha shirt only a tourist would buy. Tattoos inked both his arms. She looked above the gods scowling on his shirt and the dragons snarling on his arms, seeking traces of a young soldier in the old man's florid face, and couldn't find him. She became more aware of herself than of him, her age, her greying hair, her enfeebled position. She smiled shyly, remembering old intimacies, the knowledge of bodies.

He obviously didn't know whether to kiss her or thrust out his gnarled hand bristling with black knuckle hair. He decided on caution, or maybe he just was too disappointed, but he folded his arms across the altar of his tiki shirt. "Hello, Melba. It's been a long time."

Reprimand lurked in the greeting, but at least the quality of his voice hadn't changed. It still had an intriguing tension. A dense clump of wiry grey hair growled out of his shirt collar. She pictured him astride a motorcycle, revving the engine. She recalled that had been her first impression of him all those years ago on the USO dance floor in Waikiki, a tough guy, a biker, unconventional, free, an open road yawning wide before him. Once more, she was intrigued by him, and found she still liked the taste of uncertainty and danger. She responded softly, "Ages. I'm so sorry to hear about your wife. Sweetie always kept me posted on you."

"It was a two-way street. She always wrote me news of you." He smiled for the first time.

In the smile and eyes, Melba saw the beloved G.I. who had gone so carelessly off to Korea, positive he would marry an Island girl on his way back home, and all her old regrets came swimming back, shimmering and surprisingly impersonal.

She knew this must be difficult for him, too. She imagined him getting ready for this reunion as carefully as she did, being fastidious in personal details such as breath odor and nose hair. He probably splashed on shaving lotion, powdered under his arms and down his pants, checked himself out in a mirror, sucked in his gut, said, "Oh well," and hoped for the best. She reached out, took his vein-ridged hand, trying to ignore the dragon fangs, and was shocked to be comforted and thrilled. He turned his face to the ceiling and she knew it thrilled him, too. As if perfectly composed she said, "I'm so glad to see you, Dick. You're looking fine. A sight for sore eyes." We use cliches to cover our inadequacies, to fill the places we dare not venture. She thought of her daughter-in-law's arsenal of trite sayings, then squeezed Dick's hand and released it.

Sweetie, standing by the window with her husband, looked immensely pleased with herself. "It's almost like old times sake, yah? All we need is some music." She grabbed the remote from the tray table, and television invaded the room with an entourage of flawlessly coiffed people in nice clothes looking deadly serious about some major crisis. She changed the channel. News. "I give up." She turned it off, shrugged. "Well. Here we are all together again."

Hal said, "Except we're too old to dance."

"Speak for yourself, Honey." Sweetie raised a shoulder to him, smiling like a woman half her age and half her size.

Dick looked directly at Melba, his eyes still a brilliant blue, and said in a low voice, as if they were the only two people in the room, maybe in the world, "I've thought of you often over the years." He cleared his throat. He must have rehearsed this.

"Me, too. We had a good time, didn't we?"

Sweetie towed Hal to the door, "We're going for coffee. Be back in a jiff. Want anything? The cafeteria cookies are so *ono* – like I need them." She patted her hip as she walked out.

A desperate quiet descended on the room. Dick said, "It's been almost fifty years." A little reprimand lurked, as if she had kept him waiting on a street corner for fifty years, looking foolish, a corsage in his hands while life sauntered by.

"A lifetime." Her tone was conciliatory, a woman's tone. "Were they good years for you, Dick?"

"Mostly. I guess I can say mostly. The last few were hard. Real hard. Losing my business. Losing Connie. The kids scattered.

"I've got a daughter all the way in Singapore."

"Singapore? Cheezus." He shook his head, running a hand briefly into his hair, as if pulling might help. "And how 'bout you, Melba? How's it been for you?"

"Well, I suppose I've been as happy as anyone has a right to be. I've been a widow for seven years now."

"Does it get any easier?" It was more a plea than a question.

"Yes. I promise."

"You know, you work hard all your life and you look forward to a few carefree years -- golf, a Winnebago, maybe a cruise to Alaska or go through the canal. And bingo – one of you is gone, the business goes belly-up, and you're not only old, you're broke. I mean, I'm not exactly down and out. I got a house, a few bucks left. But it's not the way I planned things. But it's par for the course, I suppose. Sometimes I get so mad. I wonder what it's all for, anyway. Nothing. That's what."

"It's not for nothing. How many children do you have?"

"Two. Both girls. Never had a son. I would have liked one. Lori, my oldest, lives in Kansas City. Her husband's a meat packer, and the other one, Lisa, is going through another divorce. She lives in Santa Fe and makes jewelry. One of her kid's a drug addict. He cleans her out regularly. His own mother. Lisa's other kid, Candi Lee, is on permanent disability from a car accident and lives with Lisa. Nothing disabled about Candi Lee as far as I can see, except she's fat as a house, and she's mean. I'd kick her the hell out. I tell Lisa right to her face. I wouldn't stand for it. No sirree."

"It sounds like you have your hands full."

"Yeah, well, *comme ci, comme ca*. What're ya gonna do anyway? Nothin you can do."

Hoping to cheer him, or at least divert him, Melba said, "Remember our wild days in Waikiki? We were so young and crazy."

"Crazy in love." The word "love" slipped out

prematurely, before anyone could get ready for it. Love's accusations and possessiveness, expectations and power, its risky lightness had entered the room and anything was possible.

Melba reached into the drawer of her bed stand and withdrew a photograph. "Remember this?"

Dick stared at the picture of Melba in cat glasses, mangoes stuffed in her bathing suit, blowing him a kiss all those years ago. He continued to stare.

"You took it," Melba prompted.

He turned it over and read, "The Mango Queen of Waikiki."

"You wrote that."

"You kept it all these years?"

"Actually, my brother did."

"When I got your Dear John letter, Melba, I didn't care whether I lived or died. I came out of Korea with a lot of decorations. They called me a hero, but I just didn't give a monkey's ass – excuse my French."

"It was the hardest letter I ever wrote."

"Then why?"

She sighed, unable to look at him. "I was a good Japanese daughter. I obeyed my mother. Today, it might have been different."

"Today it can be different. It's not too late, Melba. I never stopped loving you."

She became alarmed. He uttered the words she had often dreamed of hearing, imagining in the dryness of routine, children at her ankles, supper half cooked, Shuzo in the yard with his hose watering the plants. She used to imagine a swashbuckling rescue by a young soldier who refused to take no for an answer and would whisk her away to the vast Mainland with all its possibilities of fulfillment and material goods.

It was a sad thing to be finally offered the rescue when you already saved yourself through simple brute endurance, and it was even sadder to confront in a man a need so secretly cultivated, so urgent and enormous that it was weakness. Dick Bower looked ravaged, used up. He wanted her to fix his life, cook his meals, nurse him. He frightened her, and fear was no longer appealing.

"I can't," she said. "For reasons too numerous and complicated to explain. There has always been, and always will be, a tender spot in my heart for you. I guess love leaves a scar that never heals. Also, as you can see, I'm a big liability. You don't want to be stuck with me."

"I'll take good care of you."

"Dick, let's leave it be. Let's keep our wonderful memories. We can dust them off and look at them whenever we want, without having to pick up after each other. Besides –" she exaggerated, "I'm already engaged. Fool that I am, I'm about to take the plunge again."

"Hal and Sweetie didn't tell me."

"They don't know yet. And please don't tell them. I don't want word getting back to my kids before I tell them. You know Sweetie."

"I feel like six kinds of a jerk." He jammed his fists into his pockets, walked to the window, his back to her.

"Dick – take that cruise through the canal. The ships are wall-to-wall with widows. Pick out a rich one. You're a genuine catch."

"Except for you." Phlegm decorated the words.

"I'm already caught."

He turned around, angry. "A day late and a dollar short. That's the story of my life."

"Then why would anyone want to share your life?" Her own rising anger caught her off guard. It was bitter and civil like a breakfast argument between two long-married and mutually disappointed people. She softened her tone, "I know you're going through a hard time right now and if you want to blame me for everything that's gone wrong because I didn't wait for you fifty years ago, then go right ahead. Be my guest. Anger gives you energy -- of this I'm sure."

He didn't answer, faced the window again.

She continued, "I've had more than my share of anger and sorrow. But you get through it. You just stick

it out and things get better. Look. We've both survived –
two arms, two legs, two eyes. That in itself is a wonder
at our age. So, no excuses -- if you want the Winnebago,
the cruise, go get them. You know, Dick …" She
realized how much he needed generosity, "When you
smile, it takes years off your face. So? What are you
waiting for? Smile."

He shrugged his shoulders, turned and smiled
reluctantly, endearingly, shaking his head.

It takes so little to please a man, just a small
compliment to his physical appearance. "There, see. You
don't look a day over fifty."

"Fifty?"

"You have to laugh a lot to look younger than
that. And here's some more free advice -- which I'm
good at, and which is hard to live with so you're lucky
you don't have to -- don't bother people with your
sorrows. They'll be eyeing the exit while you're talking.
They've got troubles enough of their own. Or if they're
happy, they won't want you raining on their parade. Tell
them your dreams instead. Dreams are more contagious
than head colds. And look at the future more than the
past, as much fun as the past was. That's one I'm still
working on."

"I'm obviously a slow learner. I always looked
back and saw you waving goodbye, blowing kisses at

me."

"Dick, you're a handsome man -- could lose a few pounds -- but basically sound. You'll be snatched up in no time."

"And as I recall, you said almost those exact words in your letter. 'You have a lot to offer.' That's what you said."

Melba wanted this over with. It had gone as far as it was going, and she was tired. She folded her hands in her lap and said as brightly as possible, "I was right then, and I'm right now. You do have a lot to offer."

"You're hard-hearted, Melba. I seen it back then. But you were so cute and so tiny … and so crazy. I thought you'd warm up if I loved you enough."

She didn't know if she was more stunned by his accusation, or by the thought that all the time they were together, he had wanted to change her, make alterations in something she had thought was such a perfect fit. She stared at him, about to tell him about their baby, but he began to speak again.

He lowered his voice, sounding discouraged and hard, "You have no compassion. It wasn't ever in your dictionary. And you're wrong about people. Some people will listen to your sorrows. They even take them on themselves and help you carry them. Connie was like that. My biggest regret, right now, is the part of my heart

I always saved for you. Connie deserved all of me."

Barely able to speak, Melba whispered, "I did that, too. I cheated my husband."

Either he didn't hear, or wasn't interested. He continued, "Sweetie's another one of the world's good people."

Relieved to move into safer territory, Melba agreed, "Sweetie is the salt of the earth."

"I bet you don't know Hal has early Alzheimer's."

"I … no. When? I mean how long has he had it?"

With starch in his voice Dick said, "They've known for almost a year."

"Why didn't Sweetie tell me?"

"That's a good question for you to ask her yourself. How come your best friend doesn't tell you what's going on in her life?"

"She could have told me. I always tell her everything."

"Yeah. Like you're getting married. You dole out to people only what you want them to have and you keep the rest to yourself. So that's what you get back -- leftovers. You know what I think? I think getting that Dear John letter from you was the luckiest thing that ever happened to me. So, thank you. That's all I got to say. Thank you. It was worth coming all the way out here just to know this. I'm finally rid of you."

If she told him about aborting his only son, she would win. She said simply, "I'm sorry."

"I'll wait outside for Hal and Sweetie."

"No need."

"I prefer to wait out there. So long, Mango Queen." He saluted, as he did once before, boarding a troop ship at Pearl Harbor.

It was all so gaudy and theatrical, she grinned. "At least I'm still the queen."

"Yeah. Good luck to your fiancé. He's gonna need it."

She was glad to see him leave.

Mama, you were right.

But his words stung.

Alzheimer's. Sweetie, you could have told me.

CHAPTER TWENTY-ONE

In which the ancient Mr. Lau Yi Ching gets his mangoes and Sachi does not get the secret mango bread recipe – but everyone else does.

In full sunshine, in the squinty light of eleven A.M., Kenji drove Melba home. She relaxed only when she heard the rhythm of the road change from the fast hollow hum of the Lunalilo Freeway to the uphill cruise of the Sixth Avenue exit. The pale blue Honda turned onto the narrow street between Sacred Hearts Academy and Saint Patrick's Church and School. On one side, girls in navy pleats and white middy blouses skipped rope under the benign gaze of stone saints. On the other, boys and girls in green uniforms ran about madly in some pattern, which like the universe, is not always apparent to the naked eye or comprehensible to the casual observer. At the corner of Waialae, Kenji turned, passing the front of Saint Patrick's where the saint of Ireland stands in green robes gazing on mountains as emerald as Erin's and two oceans away. The church parking lot was crowded. A sleek black hearse waited near the door. Melba looked away. "Aren't the Ko'olaus beautiful today?" she asked. Towering clouds crowned the jagged peaks. The valleys lay deep in their shadows, a mystery of greens, blues and lavenders. There was a tenderness about the mountains that was in contrast to their dramatic volcanic shapes. They lured, deceived and swallowed hikers with an alarming degree of regularity. They lulled the unwary into thinking that something so lovely, so adorned in trees, singing with streams and swathed in the flagrance of ginger, couldn't possibly be dangerous.

Just to gaze upon those ridges and know they were actually the tops of an immense mid-ocean range of giants that rise from the darkness of the sea floor and supported this cacophony of life was enough for Melba today. She felt intensely the quickening and sharpness of her senses, the wild joy that follows an encounter with death.

Kenji said, "I've never seen a sight more beautiful. When I was in the war, it distressed me to me to think that if I died, I'd never be buried beneath those mountains, that my bones would not be part of this island. When I think of all the Hawai'i boys who never made it home, who lie in frozen ground in France, Italy and Germany, it breaks me up. To this day."

"When you're gone, you're gone. What difference does it make? And we'll be gone soon

enough." Melba had no fear. She had been to the abyss
and back. Every moment was a gift, the swirl of cream
on the top of the cup of coffee. As they passed Zippy's,
Melba asked, "You want to stop for teri plate?"

"I think Renee made lunch."

"Renee's at the house?"

"All the kids at the house."

"What?"

"Everybody's at the house. Make pretend you're
surprised."

"But I just want to crawl into my own bed with
my own pillow."

"The whole family's so happy you're coming
home." He moved into the left lane. "We all love you."

Still looking longingly at Zippy's, and briefly
imagining a lunch of teriyaki chicken with one scoop of
creamy macaroni salad and two scoops of perfectly done
rice, she said, "I think, Kenji, you're right. It's time we
got married and set a good example for our kids."

He kept his eyes on the road, put his left blinker
on. After he executed the turn, he pulled over alongside
the Chevron station, both hands high on the steering
wheel, like a man about to be hauled out for a sobriety
test. Walk the line.

Melba sat confidently with her hands folded
prissily in her lap. "If it doesn't work out," she said,

"you can put me to sleep and bury me at Valley of the Temples."

He turned his whole body toward her, his face so sagging and dear, the sunlight glinting on his glasses. "You heard me?"

She nodded, without turning to face him.

"How much you heard while you were out?"

She slipped her arm through his, leaned her head on his shoulder and sighed, "Enough to make me cry."

"I'm so sorry. I never meant to put that burden on you. I thought you were out like a light. I thought, here's a chance to say those terrible things I saw in the war and get them out of myself without hurting anyone. I'm so sorry." He shook his head ponderously back and forth.

"It's okay, Kenji. Someday, on a day like this one, we'll take a walk on a windy beach with lots of lava rocks to bruise our feet, and I'll tell you how my father died. But not now. Not this minute. He spoiled enough of my life."

Kenji's face was in profile, the nose tall for a Japanese.

Melba waited a moment, then said with deliberate and exaggerated coyness, "You're not taking back that proposal, are you? I distinctly heard that." She teased him, risking rejection, but confident of the outcome.

He put his arm around her, "No, no. In my mind we're already married. Just like that. It's done awready. I'm just wondering where we're going to live?"

"Why, at my house, of course. I've got the mango tree."

His lips slid along her cheek until they found her mouth. His kiss was soft with a poignant tenderness that the young with years ahead of them can't imagine. "Then it's settled," he said.

*

As soon as she saw her small house with its faded yellow paint, the purple bougainvillea blazing under the porch, her chair just so by the railing, Melba took a deep breath and patted Kenji's thigh.

He said, "First thing, I think we need to paint the house white. That yellow is so old and chipped. And then I'll whack that bougainvillea under control."

Melba swallowed hard, then coughed.

"You okay?" he asked.

"Fine." The negotiations of life with a man have started. What she says now will determine the way things will go until one of them dies. "It's just that I like my yellow house. I planted the purple bougainvillea to go with it."

He put on the signal to turn into her driveway. "I always liked a nice clean white house with mock orange hedge." He waited for a car to pass before turning. "I never lived in a yellow one. It will be something new."

"I really like yellow."

"It's your house." She heard a trace of peevishness.

The door to the house flew open. Rosemary came tumbling out. "They're here, they're here."

A crowd rushed out onto the porch – Kathleen with her gangly sons towering over her; the twins, bird-like and flapping; Raymond hanging back in the shadows. Renee and Glenn brushing against each other with a new tenderness, all flowed down the steps, the space between them negligible. Lance, with the authority of his profession, eased his way forward. He opened the car door. "Mom, let me help you." He gently extracted her from the front seat.

Melba found herself a bit wobbly.

Renee took her other arm, kissing her on the cheek, "Welcome home, Mom." Her hair was damp from showering, her permanent springing in a thousand tiny curls.

As they helped her up the steps, Melba paused, craned her neck to look past Lance toward the mango tree. It looked dusty and exhausted. A few mangoes dangled way up high, all that was left of the tree's abundance. She noticed the ladder propped under the tree. "Nobody put that ladder away yet? Kids, today, I tell you. And where are my mangoes? Somebody come and strip the tree?" She smiled to let them know she was not grouchy, but greatly pleased and contented.

Renee, in the condescending tone she used with her mother, said, "Calm down, Mom. We just took the ladder out today. Lance and the kids have been picking all morning so they'd be *pau* when you got home. Isn't that what you wanted?"

Rosemary said, "And we've got them sorted the way you do, Gramma. See?"

Brown bags of mangoes were stacked all over the porch. And there on the wicker table, beside her chair, was a bowl piled with perfect mangoes, the cream of the crop. "I want to sit here a few minutes."

"We've got lunch ready," Avis announced, prepared for insult and resistance.

Hazel added, "Everything that's supposed to be hot is hot, and the cold stuff is cold."

"Mom made her killer lasagna," Rosemary said.

The child is proud. She must have inherited *haole* taste buds. "That will be lovely," Melba said, "But first I just want to sit out here a little bit."

"Actually, Mom," Renee argued, "we've got a whole spread. Everything you like, *misoyaki* butterfish, *somen* salad, *ogo* from Farmer's Market, and I made *nishime* and put in lots of *hasu* and *araimo* the way you like it – I hope. Glenn tied the *konbu* for me." She settled her mother into the porch chair, then whispered in her ear, "Glenn and I are getting married. I finally decided."

Melba clutched her hand in alarm, "Don't do it."

"But Mom, I thought that's what you wanted." Renee pulled away.

"I do. But don't marry for your mother." She drew Renee down and whispered intensely, while everyone else went inside to eat the hot things hot and the cold things cold. "When I married your father, I held myself back. I loved someone else."

"Mom."

"Baba-san wanted me to marry your father. Oh, she was a tyrant in her way. Those steely silences. You never saw that side of her. She was a sweet old Granny to you. I did my duty when I married your father. I married a nice Japanese boy. But you know what? I came to love your father deeply. He was such a fine man. But it wasn't fair to him, all those years of holding back, dreaming of a soldier I met in Waikiki."

"Mom. Not. I can't handle this."

"You may find this hard to believe, but your Auntie Sweetie and I were rebels – and we were the cat's meow."

"Auntie Sweetie I can picture."

"And what? I'm chopped liver?"

"Mom, this is scary information. I was almost a blonde. Wait – I almost didn't exist."

"Follow your heart, Renee, while you can."

"Follow my heart and I'll end up chopped liver on the Vegas strip."

"Don't marry Glenn. He's too nice. Like your father."

"For a minute I thought you were worried about me."

"Don't marry him unless you hold nothing back. That's all I'm saying."

"Mom, I'm not anything like you. I'm almost forty getting married. I know all about relationships. My generation is good at this. Yours was good at endurance."

"And a good thing for you kids."

"I think I would have married Glenn a long time ago except the pressure you put on me made me more stubborn not to marry him. I didn't want you to have the satisfaction of being right. You're always right."

"I made one big wrong decision, and it was the best one I ever made."

"Well, I know Glenn is right for me and you helped me see it by falling out of the mango tree. Almost losing you made me realize that all we really have is today, and I better quit reacting to you and take charge of my life."

The screen door opened. "Gramma, are you coming in yet? My mom's lasagna is getting cold."

A little toot of a horn interrupted them.

Renee waved, called out, "Aloha, Auntie Sweetie."

Sweetie, with the Foster Botanical Garden pinned in her hair, pointed to Melba's driveway, "I can pull in? I got two coolers."

Renee motioned her in, saying to Melba, "Auntie Sweetie always has two coolers in the car. They're built in. She never goes more than a block from the house without packing enough food to get through a nuclear winter. A trip to Hawai'i Kai is an expedition to Outer Mongolia. Ten to one she's got *kulolo*, sliced sweet potatoes, *kalua* pig and a year's supply of diet coke."

Sweetie got out of the car with her dancer's grace. Her hips move like butter, her hands fluttered to her hair, checking the garden. "Hoo-eee." She motioned to Riley and Tiernan, "You two, move your muscles over this way. These two coolers need coming out." She turned to Melba, "I made *kalua* pig – oven kind, but good, some sweet potato all sliced – and our favorite – *kulolo*." She pointed, saying to the boys, "Leave the coolers on the porch. Juice and diet coke. Help yourselfs."

She floated up the steps, adrift in her floral mu'umu'u, kissing everyone. She knelt beside Melba, "How you, Dear?"

"Glad to be home." Melba took her hand and asked quietly, "How's Hal?"

"You know?" Her eyes filled with tears.

"Dick told me."

"We put Dick on the plane yesterday. Hal told him to give our aloha to Connie. He forgot she was dead. It's going to be so hard, Melba, losing Hal little by little, watching him …"

"I'll be there for you, Sweetie. Every step of the way. I promise." They clung to each other's hands, heads together, knowing the great cost of bearing and losing life, and the immense consolation of doing it all in the intimate company of female friends.

Renee came over, "Hey, you two. This is supposed to be a happy day."

Melba smiled, squeezed Sweetie's hand. "Renee and Glenn are getting married."

Sweetie dabbed her eyes, rallied into the cheerful facade always expected of her. "Congratulations, Girl. It's about time."

"Get her to come in and eat, Auntie."

Melba allowed herself to be raised from the chair by Sweetie's arm and swept into the house. "Oh my," she said.

Crepe paper streamers hung from the ceiling. Banks of orchids cheered every end table, corner and the coffee table. A computer-generated banner fluttered across the room, proclaiming, "Welcome Home, Grandma." Pink ponies and unicorns pranced across the paper. Melba clutched her hands to her chest, as if to pray. "Oh my. Oh my. It's so – beautiful."

"You like the sign, Grandma? Rosemary asked. "Tiernan made it on the computer – but I added the artwork."

"It's lovely. I'm flub the dub."

Avis complained, "The hot food's getting cold, and the cold stuff's melting."

Renee said, "Auntie Avis and Auntie Hazel did most of the cooking. Come see. They made baked ham with black cherry sauce, spinach salad with chutney dressing, all the sushi, the avocado Jell-O mold, *li hing* fruit."

Sweetie busied herself rearranging the buffet table to accommodate her Saran-wrapped platters.

Kathleen asked, "Can we hold hands for a prayer?" She always did that. Melba expected it, even liked it. When everyone shuffled into position, Kathleen bowed her head, "Dear Lord, we thank you for the bounty you have set before us. We thank you that our mother is home safely in our midst. Bless the doctors and nurses who attended her. We thank you for the love we share in this home. Please bless our conversation and help us to be a gift to each other. Amen."

Everyone insisted Melba and Kenji go to the buffet first. Melba said, "There's only one thing missing – mango bread." Everyone laughed. She instructed Renee, "Go get my old accordion file from the shelf. Look under soup."

"Soup?"

"If I filed my mango bread recipe under bread, someone would find it. It's under soup."

"Here it is, here it is," Renee waved it above her head.

Melba, in the meantime, loaded up her plate and walked toward the porch, "Anyone who wants can copy."

"After lunch," Avis begged. "Please. Everything will get cold."

"Or melt," Hazel added. "The Jell-O mold is sliding already." She was close to despair. Jell-O was her specialty.

One by one, as they fixed their plates, the family came out to sit on the porch. Someone put some

Hawaiian CDs on the player, Keali`i Riechel, *Kawaipunahele,* lush and merciful. Sweetie sang along between bites.

Renee asked, "Dance, Auntie?"

"Later. First *ai ai.*"

Raymond sat near Melba. "When the orchids are finished blooming, I'll come and get them and bring more, in bloom."

"Raymond, that's so thoughtful of you. Are you sure you want to leave them? I kill orchids, you know."

"Just enjoy them. "I'll be stopping by to take care of them."

Rosemary pointed to the road. "Look, there's Uncle Peter and Auntie Sachi." She waved, yelled, "Hi, Uncle Peter." She addressed no one in particular, "He's looking for a parking space."

Melba demanded, "Where's that mango bread recipe?"

"Kathleen's got it," Renee answered. "She's copying it."

"Well go tell her hide it. I'm not sharing it with Sachi. She won't last and the recipe will go outside the family when Peter dumps her. They'll be serving my mango bread at Zippy's before I know it."

"I like Auntie Sachi's clothes," Rosemary defended. "She's pretty, and she always smells nice."

Avis, concentrating on her plate, muttered with grim satisfaction, "If I had her money, I'd have clothes like that and French perfume. You know what she told me on New Year's when she had a little too much to drink?" Avis checked to make sure she had everyone's attention before continuing, "Sachi said that when she got divorced from her previous husband, she sold the house and invested ten grand in her body. She had a face lift, butt lift, tummy tuck and breast implants."

Renee said, "Hey, it worked. She snagged Peter."

Hazel added, "It won't last. Their relationship is superficial."

Melba said, "So is Peter. She's perfect for him. And here they come."

Sachi was stunning in immaculate white pants, an obviously expensive long sleeved white tunic printed with gold anchors, and she carried a quilted leather Chanel purse. Peter clutched a fruit basket. She greeted everyone, kissing, grabbing hands, "How nice to see you. We can't stay. We leave for Kuala Lumpur tonight and I'm only partially packed. Peter is involved in a new resort there with the Sultan of Sarawak. We'll be staying at the palace. Then we go to Thailand for shopping. The last time we were in Bangkok, Peter found a Giorgio Armani jacket for eighty dollars. Can you believe? No label, of course. We know it's Armani because we saw it in Liberty House later for seven hundred and fifty, same fabric, the exact jacket." She kissed Melba on the cheek, "Welcome home, Dear."

Peter kissed her on the other cheek. "Are you okay? Let me know if you need anything."

"A Bangkok ruby would be nice."

He laughed nervously. "The Sultan has precious jewels studded into mosaics on his walls. In the old days they released tigers to prowl the halls at night to make sure nobody picked at the walls."

"I hope Sachi doesn't have to use the bathroom in the middle of the night. She'll end up as cat food."

"Now they've got security guards instead of tigers."

"Good. They can be bribed. Get me a ruby or two. And make yourself a plate."

"My mom made her killer lasagna."

"It's cold by now," Avis said smugly.

Melba was merciful. "Run it in the microwave."

"It'll be fine," Peter said, and ruffled Rosemary's hair. As he and Sachi went inside to get food, all the women silently and expertly appraised Sachi's clothes and jewelry, and looked hopefully for signs her facelift might be slipping.

Hazel sniffed her wake. "Oscar."

"Oscar?" her twin echoed.

"De la Renta. The perfume."

Rosemary offered, "Do you want seconds on the lasagna, Grandma? I'll nuke it in the microwave for you."

"No thank you, Dear. Although it's very good."

Kathleen startled Melba with her raucous laugh. "It's an old Bronx recipe. I learned it from my mother who learned it from our next-door neighbor. My mom had to go and ask this Sicilian woman who couldn't speak a word of English to teach her to cook because me and my brothers and sisters used to go sit on her back stoop every afternoon and swoon from the smells coming out of her kitchen. So, this lasagna is the real thing. Even when eaten with chopsticks." She laughed loudly again.

She can't help it, Melba thought. Loud is how she was raised.

Kenji asked, "You tired?"

"Yes." Inexplicably, she almost began to cry. She gathered herself and said, "But before I nap, I'm going to divide up the mangoes."

Rosemary took her plate away and Melba turned to the bowl on the table. "These are beautiful mangoes. Perfection. But there was a white Pirie. Anyone see it?"

Lance answered, "It's in there, Mom. It was the first one I picked. That's the first white Pirie I saw since

Dad died."

"It's the one I was reaching for when I fell." She shuffled the mangoes in the bowl, handling each carefully, reverently. "Ah, here it is."

Lance smiled broadly, "I wanted you to be surprised when you came to it."

Melba held up the white mango. It was smaller than the other mangoes, but its pale iridescent skin glowed softly in her hand.

Avis was not impressed. "The white ones are so sour."

Looking directly at Kathleen, Melba smiled and said, "Never mind. They're beautiful -- and perfect for pickle. Dear Shuzo -"

Kathleen interrupted, "God rest his soul."

"Shuzo always reminded me," Melba continued, "that it was under a mango tree that the Buddha rested and found tranquility." She sat back. "I think your father always suspected I married him for that tree. He said that in the Hindu religion, the mango symbolizes love."

"Just one bite of a mango and you know there's a God up there," Kathleen lifted an arm toward the sky, "who loves us."

"The tree is related to poison ivy, you know." Melba couldn't resist. "Shuzo said the leaves are toxic."

"So is love." Kathleen's hearty laughter was

contagious. Everyone joined in.

Melba gently rolled the white mango in her hand then gave it to Lance. "You have this one. I think your father sent it." She then took another mango from the bowl. "A gold Pirie. Observe its blush, the firm softness. The touch of purple. This is for Kathleen." Melba passed it to her in a ritual they all knew well. Melba continued, "Ah, look at the perfect shape of this one, the little golden nipple. This is *Mapulehu* and it's for Sweetie." She caressed it from the stem down and awarded it to her friend. Next, she lifted out a Hayden. "How pretty, all the little gold speckles in the crimson. Glenn, take this to your mother. Oh, and here we have the Honey Manila, small and flat and smooth as butter. Sachi, you take this, for the journey." She went through the whole basket in that manner, as she did every year. On this occasion, however, the event was mesmerizing as if the whole universe was poised in perfect order for the distribution of Melba's mangoes.

Renee said, "Some people just give you a bag of mangoes. Our mother bestows them. And you don't just say thanks and put the bag in the refrigerator. You are expected, when she comes with the mangoes, to sit down and appreciate each one as she takes it from the bag."

Melba was pleased to have lived long enough to become an eccentric in the eyes of her offspring.

Lance said, "Mom, you forgot our Manoa Yamada cousins."

"They are not getting mangoes this year."

"Why not?"

"When we visited last New Year's Day, my cousin Ryozo's wife, Helen, called Kenji Shuzo. She knows better."

"Mom, it was just a mistake. She's old."

"I am the Mango Queen. I decide who gets mangoes and who does not. The Manoa Yamadas do not." She gripped the arms of her chair, squinting toward the street. "Oh look, there goes Mr. Lau Yi Ching. Renee, invite him over."

"Mom, no."

Melba pursed her lips, "Why not? He probably saved my life."

"He gives me the creeps. That's all."

"Then, Riley, go take him this small bag of mangoes. Hurry."

The old man, upon receipt of his package, turned and briefly bowed his wiry frame, then scurried away, nimble and quick as always.

Melba announced, "I'm tired. Now I'll take a nap. And I'm trusting you kids to divide up the rest of the mangoes fairly. But not one to the Manoa Yamadas. And Kathleen, make sure Sachi doesn't see the mango bread recipe."

"Oh." Kathleen blushed. "I already gave her a copy."

Melba glared at her freckled daughter-in-law. "She'll sell it to Zippy's."

Renee intervened, "It's okay, Mom. The only thing Sachi ever reads is price tags."

Melba started to get out of the chair. Kenji leaped to help her. "I hope you're right," she said, heading for the bedroom, "or Boy Scouts will be selling Zippy's mango bread for fund-raiser."

Peter and Sachi came out of the house. Sachi said in a sing-song voice, "We've got to run. I've got my mangoes." She patted her Chanel purse, "and I've got that secret mango bread recipe."

Melba was again surprised by tears, by a sudden compassion for Sachi, so gamely defying her years, surviving on diminished tools, knowing her husband's marital record could lead to doom and a walk-up apartment in Makiki at any moment. "Enjoy." Melba embraced her. She then looked around, tears embarrassing her. "Everyone make plate to go. So much food. So much love."

*

Later, as Renee and Kathleen did the dishes in the narrow kitchen, Kathleen said, "I was shocked to see how much oil and sugar the famous mango bread recipe calls for.

"It's a good thing mangoes don't come all year. We'd be blimps with cholesterol up the yin-yang."

"You know how I like them best?" Kathleen swirled the sponge in a casserole dish and ran it under the faucet. "I treat mangoes like tomatoes -- dump them in tossed salad -- a little olive oil and nice mild balsamic vinegar. That would be a better way for Mom to eat mangoes than with all that sugar and *shoyu*. I'll have to get her a salad spinner. She doesn't eat enough greens."

"She told me that when she was young she almost married a soldier in Waikiki. Just think -- I might have been a blonde."

"You're kidding."

"She was the cat's meow -- an exact quote." Renee laughed as she toweled the casserole dish. "Did you see how upset she was that Sachi got the mango bread recipe."

Kathleen let out one of her whooping laughs. She laughed so hard she clutched the sink and crossed her legs. "You'll never guess what I did. I can't believe I did it." She gasped and laughed, tears running down her cheeks. "I'm so bad. I don't know whatever prompted me."

"What? What?" Renee laughed although she

had no idea what she was laughing about. "Tell me."

Kathleen threw herself into a chair, buried her face in her hands. "I've got a devil in me for sure. And I'll burn in hell for this one."

"Come on -- tell. You're killing me."

Kathleen dissolved in laughter again and finally managed to get out, "I – I put an extra cup of vegetable oil into the copy of the recipe I made for Sachi."

Renee screeched in joy, "Wait til Mom hears this."

"I heard it." Melba leaned on the doorjamb. "I couldn't help but hear it. You two would wake the dead." Then she smiled. She sat beside her daughter-in-law and cupped her age- spotted hand over Kathleen's freckled one. "Now. Get out the flour, the raisins, the walnuts and bring me the mangoes to slice. We are making bread."

MANGO BREAD RECIPE FROM THE MANGO

QUEEN OF WAIKIKI

2 cups flour
2 tsp baking soda
2 tsp cinnamon
½ tsp salt
1/4 cup coarsely chopped walnuts nuts
1 cup vegetable oil
1 tsp vanilla
1 ½ cups sugar
2 cups mango in hefty chunks
3 eggs
½ cup raisins

Sift flour, salt, soda and cinnamon together. Make a well in dry ingredients in mixing bowl. Add nuts, oil, vanilla, sugar, mangoes, eggs and raisins. Mix well and pour into well-greased 9x5x3 inch loaf pan. Let stand 20 minutes before baking. Bake at 350 degrees F for 1 hour.

241

ACKNOWLEDGEMENTS

OKAGE-SAMA DE

This work of fiction would not have been possible without the many true stories told to me over many years by family and friends who lived through the attack on Pearl Harbor, Hawaii, December 7, 1941. I wish I could have woven all their stories, the profound, tragic, funny and weird into my tale. I was most interested in how the war changed life in Hawaii forever, especially for Japanese Americans. To shape my book I spent days in the archives of the local newspapers, the *Honolulu Advertiser* and the *Honolulu Star Bulletin* (now merged as the *Honolulu Star Advertiser*) reading the fine on-the-ground reporting of the events of the war. I also visited the Arizona Memorial where World War II began for

America, and the battle ship *Missouri* in Pearl Harbor where the war ended. I traveled to Japan to visit the Nagasaki Atomic Bomb Museum.

My dear friends Jodi Belknap, Mary Bell, Joseph Bonfiglio, Carol Catanzariti, Thelma Chang, April Coloretti, Clemence McClaren and Kaui Philpotts were faithful readers and helped the Mango Queen with their wise critiques and tea.

I was fortunate enough to have Vern Turner, a prolific author with nine novels to his credit, as my editor again, after he guided my debut novel, *Lion's Way* to publication in 2022. Savant Publisher, Kendrick Simmons loved The Mango Queen into life.

Chapter Seven of the Mango Queen was originally published in the inflight magazine of Aloha Airlines, *Spirit of Aloha.*

My family deserves a deep bow for putting up with me during the writing process, for the meals and emergency runs to See's Candy in Kahala Mall. I am especially grateful to my husband, Joe, who supports me even when I seem more married to my keyboard. My children, Daisy, Clare and David have always respected my writing time with admirable restraint. I wish I could say the same thing about our poodle, Mikimoto, but she consoled and amused me and gave me an excuse to quit the book and go to the beach.

The Mango Queen's mango bread recipe is actually our treasured family recipe, acquired half a century ago from the Yuan family.

Okage-sama de. Because of you...

.

Made in the USA
Columbia, SC
22 September 2024

42837925R00135